BON REPOS

COLETTE

JACQUELINE

MAKE-BELIEVE

"STOP, YOU YOUNG RASCALS, STOP!"

MAKE-BELIEVE

by

ELIZABETH GOUDGE

Illustrated by

C. WALTER HODGES

GERALD DUCKWORTH & CO. LTD.

3 Henrietta Street, London, W.C. 2

PRINTED IN GREAT BRITAIN BY
WYMAN AND SONS, LTD., LONDON, FAKENHAM AND READING

CONTENTS

CHAPTER   PAGE

    I.   MAKE-BELIEVE   9

   II.   THE WELL OF SAINT GEORGE . . 37

  III.   RESCUE ON THE ISLAND . . . 65

  IV.   THE NEW MOON 91

   V.   PICNIC WITH ALBERT 116

  VI.   DOING GOOD 140

 VII.   THE FORESTERS' RIDE 161

VIII.   MIDNIGHT IN THE STABLE . . . 198

A*

LIST OF ILLUSTRATIONS

BON REPOS . . . . . *Endpapers*

"STOP, YOU YOUNG RASCALS, STOP!" *Frontispiece*

PAGE

"NOW YOUR WIVES, CHILDREN AND CATTLE ARE
AT MY MERCY!" 15

"ENTER," SAID A SHRILL, QUAVERING OLD VOICE . 51

IN THE RUE LIHOU 67

"'ERE, MR. 'IGGINS," HE GASPED, "YOU COME 'ERE
AND 'AVE A LOOK AT THIS" . . . 101

". . . TAKE IT BACK WHERE IT CAME FROM" . 127

AT THE END OF TEN MINUTES THE SACK WAS
FULL 151

IT WAS THE CROWNING GLORY OF A ROUND
GREEN HILL 169

MIDNIGHT IN THE STABLE 229

Chapter One

MAKE-BELIEVE

IT was one of those intoxicating days when all the best people go mad; and they agreed afterwards that they had, all of them, gone quite mad. . . . For hawthorn petals streamed in the wind, the sun and the rain were flying, and the smell of wet red wallflowers filled the whole world. . . . So how could one help it?

Eight-year-old Colin du Frocq was the first to wake that morning. He flung back his patchwork counterpane, bounded out of bed, and rushing to the window flung it wide open, shaking hundreds of wet drops off the leaves of the passion flower that clambered round it. Leaning out he looked, sniffed, and listened. The whole of him seemed vibrating to the magic of the day: his tumbled dark hair and white nightshirt ruffled by the wind, his dark eyes that shone and sparkled, his freckled nose wrinkling like a rabbit's, and his beautiful ears, shaped like a fawn's and lying very flat against his head, trembling as do the ears of all wild things whose hearing is acute. . . . And certainly that day was enough to make the stolidest vibrate. . . . Such a shining before the eyes of golden sunshine, sparkling raindrops all in a row upon every twig and wet leaves silver-sheeted; such scents of drenched earth, flowers,

and the salt sea; such a singing of birds in the bushes
and wind in the trees, clear and distinct against the
muffled roar of waves breaking upon the beach below
the cliff.

It was one of those days when the man with a ship
sets sail for the skyline, the man with a horse mounts
it and gallops toward the horizon, and the man who has
dreamed a dream, no matter how crazy, gives chase
that it may come true.

Colin had neither ship nor horse, but he had a pair
of strong brown legs, and his head was packed with
dreams. . . . So many of them that it was difficult to
know which one to take out and run after. . . . However,
the great thing on a day like this was to run; one would
discover where to and what after when one was actually
running.

He leaped from the window and plunged into his
morning's toilet. He decided that there was no point
in washing; he would so soon be dirty again that it
would be sheer waste of time; but he cleaned his teeth
because his toothpaste tasted good and if swallowed
did quite a lot to assuage the pangs of hunger, and
flattened out his rumpled hair with a comb dipped in
the water jug before he dragged on his patched dark-
blue knickerbockers and jersey. Then, his shoes in his
hand, he crept barefoot out of his little room and down
the winding uncarpeted staircase of the old farmhouse.
He gained the stone-floored hall and was across it in a
flash and straining in something of a panic to turn the
great key noiselessly in the front door; for if Mother or
Father or the girls were to wake up and catch him he

would be haled back to his room and washed and re-brushed, and all the precious minutes between dawn and breakfast would be wasted upon the banalities of the toilet.

But the key turned with no more than the tiniest protesting squeak, and he was out in the cobbled court-yard, blinking at the sun. This farmhouse where he lived, built not far from a rocky cliff top on an island in the English Channel, was very old, built of grey granite and roofed with weather-stained red tiles. It took up the north side of the courtyard, the other three being protected by the stables to the west and by thick old walls to south and east that had been built in medieval times to keep out enemies. A wide doorway in the east wall, that had lost its door but was still crowned by its original immense lintel of solid stone, led into the lane and in the south wall a strong oak door led into the flower garden. These two were the only entrances to a home that must once have been as impregnable as a fortress.

Yet now, at the end of the nineteenth century, the farmhouse was called Bon Repos, and the strutting pigeons in the courtyard and the rustling leaves of the passion flower that climbed about the windows spoke of nothing but peace.

And a thousand pities, too, Colin thought. Who wanted peace? For himself he liked excitement and the clash of arms. He wished he had lived in the days when Pirates beached their boats in the Bay of the Gulls below Bon Repos, and came storming up the cliff to plunder and steal. . . . Now that would have been something like. . . .   Terrified peasants, with their pigs, chickens, and cows, would have taken refuge inside the courtyard while Colin, Father, Mother, and the girls, armed with clubs and daggers, would have stood in the wide doorway, under the huge stone lintel, and defended their home to the death.   The lane outside would have run red with blood and the mound of corpses outside the door would have reached as high as the top of the hedge. . . .   Colin, scampering down the lane in question, sighed for the glories that were past.

Yet, what is imagination for if not to transport one to where one would be?   It needed only a slight mental readjustment, and a moment's pause to cut a stout stick from the hedge, and Colin was back in the great and bloody days, running dagger in hand toward the cliffs to see if the news brought by a peasant was true and the Pirates were in sight.

The land ended in a sandy path that led to the edge of the cliff, and Colin went leaping and careering like a mad thing over the short sweet turf, and in and out between the gorse bushes that filled the air with a hot smell that was the very scent of sunshine, until the path ended at a great flat rock from which the cliff fell sheer away to the Bay of the Gulls below.

Here he stood and shouted for joy.   The earth was green and the sea was blue and the great white gulls were crying and circling over his head.   The wind seemed to have blown the whole surface of the world to white foam.   Little white-capped waves were frisking on the sea, every hedge was a froth of hawthorn, and white clouds raced across the sky.   Every now and then a silver shower came by on the wind, but so small and so swift that its passing was only an added delight to the glory of the day.

Abruptly Colin stopped shouting and remembered what he was here for. Transforming the dagger into a telescope he clapped it to one eye and raked the seas. . . . Nothing. . . . It was disappointing until he remembered that just round a jutting headland of rock was Breton Bay with its fishing hamlet. The enemy had without doubt put in there first to loot the cottages, but they would be turning their attention to Bon Repos at any moment now. In a few minutes, if he listened, he would hear the rattle of oars in rowlocks and a man's voice singing the Pirates' song.

Nevertheless when he did hear them he was a bit disconcerted and suffered from a slight prickly sensation all over the surface of his body. It was a little difficult to make out if he really *was* hearing them, for the jolly song was hardly distinguishable from that other song the wind was singing in his ears, and the rattle of oars was almost lost in the breaking of waves over the rocks. . . . In fact he could not make up his mind about it until a rowing boat suddenly rounded the headland and came tumbling over the top of a wave right into the Bay of the Gulls.

"Hi! You there! You'll be smashed on the rocks!"

Colin, sure-footed as some mountain animal, came scrambling down the steep dangerous cliff path in a tearing hurry, for the Pirate in the boat, a handsome fair-haired person in a blue shirt, who was carolling cheerfully at the top of his voice, was taking apparently not the slightest notice of where he was going.

"Mind! Look out!" yelled Colin, dancing up and down where the ripples came frilling in over the ribbed golden sand. "Look where you're going, you owl!"

The man, still singing, turned his head over his shoulder, winked at Colin, and steered his boat with superb skill between two weed-covered rocks into the calm water beyond.

Colin fell silent, struck dumb with admiration. This man, though a stranger to him, was nevertheless no mean sailor, and one, moreover, who seemed to understand the rocks and currents round the Island like a native. . . . Colin kicked off his shoes and dashed into the sea to help beach the boat. . . . It was not until the thing was done that he realized the enormity of his behaviour.

"Look at me helping you to get the boat in, and you a Pirate!" he exclaimed in annoyance.

"Why didn't you put a bullet through me when I rounded those rocks?" asked the Pirate. "Bit absent-minded, weren't you? Now your wives, children, and cattle are at my mercy!" And he made a dash for the steep path up the cliff. He was young, tall, and finely made, and he ran fast, but Colin could run yet faster and was there before him, brandishing the one-time telescope which had turned without any difficulty at all into a long, slender rapier with a cruel point.

"Advance one yard further at your peril!" he growled.

"We'll fight it out, shall we?" suggested the Pirate

"NOW YOUR WIVES, CHILDREN AND CATTLE ARE AT
MY MERCY!"

15

pleasantly.   "You couldn't have a better place for a
duel than this cove.   Nice flat sandy surface.   Private.
Good, strengthening sea air.   At twenty paces, shall
we say?   With rapiers?"

They returned to the stretch of golden sand, and the
Pirate stood proudly flexing his muscles while Colin
stepped out the paces.

"To the death?" he asked.

"Oh, well," deprecated the Pirate, "it's surely a
pity to be dead on a day like this.   What do you say
to the first one to draw blood taking the other one
prisoner?"

"On guard!" said Colin briefly.

The Pirate took a pipe from his pocket, gave it a
flourish that transformed it instantly into a rapier even
deadlier than Colin's, gave a strange, high, excited
cry, flung back his leonine head, and lunged.

Now there is only one grown-up in two thousand who
has the true gift of make-believe.   A good many of
them, poor well-meaning creatures, are quite prepared
to go down on all fours as a tiger, or stand upright and
paw the air as a polar bear, but they seem quite unable
to shed their own identity.   They are not a bear at all;
they are only Uncle Henry trying to look like one.
The air of condescension, or of embarrassment, or the
silly fatuous smile they put on for the occasion, spoils
the whole thing. . . .   But one man in two thousand
upon this earth is a man of faith, his belief a wizard's
wand of creation that can make flowers blossom on a
dung heap and awake the echo of trumpets from the
dust of a battle fought a thousand years ago. . . .   And

the Proud Pirate was one of that rare company; one of those fortunate ones who never grow up.

It was therefore a grand fight that was fought in the Bay of the Gulls, a swift, clean, splendid fight that only the gulls saw, and the white waves frisking on the blue sea and the white clouds scudding across the sky. . . . They enjoyed it thoroughly. . . . The waves dashed in as close as they could to watch, and the gulls, giving wild cries of encouragement, circled nearer and nearer. They had seen this fight often before, of course, for this was not the first time in the history of the Island that an Islander had defended his strip of earth against an invader, but they had never seen so splendid a pair of fighters: the tall fair-haired man who lunged with the grace of a practiced fencer and the lithe, dark-haired boy who fought with the agility and dash of all valorous sons of the morning. . . . Yet there was no doubt as to where the Island's sympathy lay, for when an agonized cry of *"Touché!"* rang across the bay, and the Proud Pirate dropped on one knee on the sand, the gulls screamed in ecstasy and the laughing waves tossed their foam right up into the air in their joy.

Colin tied his victim's hands behind him with a piece of fishy string that he found in his pocket and propelled him up the steep path to the cliff top. It was a merciful thing that the Pirate was as sure-footed as Colin himself or there would most certainly have been an accident.

Victor and vanquished walked together between the gorse bushes on the cliff top and down the lane to Bon

Repos. The Proud Pirate had now become a Pitiful Prisoner who walked with head bowed and feet dragging. . . . Colin glanced sideways at him out of the corners of his eyes. . . . Make-believe is all very well, but the misery of the man beside him was really making him feel most uncomfortable.

"It's a nice day," he remarked brightly.

There was no answer; only a muffled groan.

Colin walked through the old doorway and across the courtyard in a painful silence. None of the family was about yet, he was thankful to see. Over the stables was an empty loft where they kept their apples, when they had any, reached by an outside stone staircase, French fashion, and up this he led his prisoner.

The loft was a delightful place and had the proper loft smell of clean horses, hay, apples, and sunshine. There were still a few rosy apples left on the shelves, and there was a mound of hay on the floor that simply invited one to lie down on it with a book. High up in the wall was a tiny square window through which the sunshine fell in long golden beams. . . . For just a moment the Pitiful Prisoner raised his head and gave an appreciative sniff; then he lowered it again, abandoned to his misery.

Colin, still feeling most uncomfortable, untied his hands, crept out of the door, locked it firmly on the outside, and pocketed the key. . . . But the sound of it turning in the lock seemed suddenly to bring the prisoner to himself. He gave a loud yelp and leaped like a kangaroo for the door.

18

"Hi, you young devil!" he shouted through the keyhole. "You've locked me in!"

Colin's pity suddenly changed to indignation. "What did you expect?" he demanded. "We agreed that the one who got the worst of the fight should be the captive of the other. And if you say we didn't you're a liar!"

"I don't say we didn't," said the Prisoner hotly. "I merely wish to remark that if you leave me here too long it will be deuced awkward for me. I happen to be a busy man."

"All right," soothed Colin. "Just stay there while I have breakfast.... You've got the apples for yours.... Good-bye." And he went scuttling off down the steps and across the courtyard to the farm-house.

Everyone was happy at breakfast, for it was Saturday and a whole holiday. They sat round the table in the big kitchen and ate and drank and laughed and blinked at the sunshine. André du Frocq, a gentle bearded little man who farmed badly but wrote poetry so exquisitely that he was already, even in his lifetime, becoming almost famous, glanced benignly round the table at his family.... His tall, dark-haired beautiful wife Rachell, his four young daughters, the clever Michelle, fascinating golden-haired Peronelle, pretty Jacqueline, and fat little baby Colette; and last but not least his son Colin.... A charming family, he thought. He glowed with pride and happiness until Toinette the maid, entering suddenly with fresh coffee, brought a

19

piece of news that shattered everyone's joy into fragments.

"M'sieur! M'dame!" she cried, setting the coffee-pot upon the table with such a crash that the coffee spurted out. "One of the sergeants at the Fort has been murdered! Ah, *mon Dieu!* What a terrible thing to happen on our Island! *Mon Dieu!* That I should live to see it!"

It was indeed a terrible and unusual thing, for the Island was considered by its Islanders to be an abode of peace where no harm stirred. The du Frocqs sat as though turned to stone, cups arrested midway to their lips and eyes staring.

"Who told you?" gasped Rachell at last.

"The baker. This very minute."

"When did it happen?" demanded André.

"Last night, M'sieur. They found the poor man flat on his face on the floor, as dead as a door-nail from a blow on the head."

"Who did it?" gasped Peronelle.

"That young English soldier who sang so well at the Christmas concert at the Fort. He'd had words with the Sergeant in the morning and then maybe had a drop to drink in the afternoon. They all hated that Sergeant. A hard man, he was."

"Have they caught the soldier?" asked Michelle.

"No, Mamselle, but they are looking for him all over the Island. A good-looking man, they say, tall and fair. He's handy with a boat, too, so he might be hiding in one of the bays." And clucking to herself in mingled horror and enjoyment Toinette took the empty coffee pot and decamped to the scullery.

A terrible blight fell upon the du Frocqs, for they were a tender-hearted and sensitive family. They could eat and drink no more, and a shadow passed over the face of the sun. . . . Fat little Colette lifted up her voice and wept.

But Colin felt worse than any of them. The key of the loft, that lay in his pocket, seemed burning a hole through his knickerbockers to his leg. . . . A good-looking man, tall and fair. A singer who was handy with a boat. . . . What on earth was he going to do?

André and his children always spent fine Saturday mornings working in the garden, and to the children it was the happiest time in the whole week. They all had their own little gardens, and while they weeded and watered and planted André would tell them stories, play with them, laugh with them, and tease them. He was an incomparable father, if slightly over-indulgent.

But to-day, though the bluebells poured over the brown earth in an azure flood of glory, the girls' talk halted, and André in his story-telling suffered from an inability to remember what happened next. Colin, beset by his own private problem, wrestled with weeds in the path and heard not one word of what the rest of them were saying.

Of one thing he was certain; he was not going to hand over his dear Pirate, that bloody and incomparable fighter, into the hands of justice. The Sergeant, they said, had been a hard man, and doubtless the Pirate, annoyed with him, had been suddenly overtaken by a fit of temper and had hit out hard. Colin himself had often been overtaken in that way, and it was doubtless only good luck that no one he had hit had died. When he was older, and his biceps firmer, probably they *would* die, and then he would find himself in as awkward a position as the Pirate's.

The difficulty was to know how to help the Pirate to escape. Colin thought it would be best to leave him where he was until dark and then put him in his boat and let him row himself across to France. . . . But the sea was rough, and it was miles and miles to France. . . . Alternatively he might be put down the well for the next few days, or inside the copper with the lid on, or in some other hiding place less obvious than the loft until the hue and cry were over. He was still worrying most dreadfully about it all when Rachell came sailing down the path, most incongruously dressed in her new violet silk and her spangled bonnet, flushed with righteous indignation and looking superb.

"André!" she cried, regarding her grubby, perspiring husband with a good deal of disfavour. "Have you *no* memory?"

"What, dear?" asked André mildly.

"Have you forgotten that this is the day of the Luncheon and Reception?"

"What Luncheon and Reception?"

"André!" gasped his wife, tears of rage springing to her beautiful eyes. "The Reception at the Guildhall for Rupert Falaise!"

"Oh," said André. "Dear me, yes. It had slipped my memory."

Rupert Falaise was an Islander who had left the Island as a boy and crossed the sea to seek his fortune. The sons of the Island had to do that, even though it broke their hearts to do it, for their land was too little a land to support them all. Rupert had been lucky. Far away in London he had become a well-known actor. The Island was told, though having known Rupert as an exceedingly grubby small boy it could hardly believe it, that in England they put up his name in coloured lights outside the theatre where he was playing, and that people would stand for hours in the rain just to catch a sight of him. . . . The more fools they, said the Islanders.

But they were nevertheless proud of Rupert, and now that he had condescended to return to his birthplace, in search of a holiday and a little peace and quiet, they were staging a gargantuan Luncheon and Reception in the Guildhall and proposed to confer upon him a mysterious honour which they called the Freedom of the Island. . . . Upon Rupert Falaise, who as a little boy had known all there was to know about the Island's freedom, running with the wind and shouting to the sun and down upon the shore standing knee-deep to watch the waves come in.

"We've been invited because of your poetry, of course," triumphed Rachell. "The first bit of recognition the Island has ever shown you. And now you're not ready! Toinette said you had dressed early and gone to your study and I find you out here not even clean! We shall be terribly late. You're hopeless, darling, perfectly hopeless!"

She put her best lace handkerchief to the corner of her eye very cautiously, so as not to crush the handkerchief, and André, terribly contrite, rubbed his earthy hands up and down his gardening trousers and sighed. . . . Then a happy thought came to him and he smiled his charming smile.

"Need we go?" he asked.

"Go?" stormed Rachell. "Of course we must go! I've got my new dress on."

"I hate these crushes," sighed André. "And at these huge affairs no one knows if you are there or not."

"They know if *I'm* there or not!" retorted Rachell. And she spoke the truth. Owing to her beauty and her considerable conversational facility she was not one of those who are overlooked.

The children flung down their gardening tools and listened with unconcealed delight. . . . A disagreement between the parents was as good as a circus any day. . . . Even Colin forgot his problem and jigged joyously from foot to foot, muttering: "Go on, Mother! Stick it, Father!"

"But we don't personally know Rupert Falaise," objected André.

"Then it's high time we did," said Rachell.

"Why?" asked André.

"He has Immense Influence," said Rachell. "He might get your play put on."

Now André had recently written a superb drama in verse, in five acts of four scenes each, beginning with a chariot fight and ending with a procession of elephants, which he was most anxious to see upon the London stage. . . . The difficulty was to know how to get it there.

"Er—yes," said André hesitantly. "But I can't exactly buttonhole him without an introduction and —er——"

"Leave it to me," said Rachell firmly. "Have you ever known me fail to get an introduction when I wanted one? And how many more times am I to tell you that it's not a bit of use you writers skulking about in the background and being too shy to go anywhere? If you want to Get On you must Meet People. . . . Now come along, darling. If we don't hurry we shall get no lunch at all."

She led him off in triumph, and the children, giggling happily, returned to their gardening.

It was not until the sound of the carriage wheels that were bearing their parents to town had died away that Colin suddenly remembered the Captive Criminal.

"Gosh!" he said, and dropped his spade.

"What's the matter?" asked Peronelle. "Hurt yourself?"

Colin, arms akimbo, looked at the girls and wondered if he could trust them. He was averse to telling secrets to women, experience having taught him it was better not, but he was so floored by his problem that he felt he must set fresh brains to work upon it.

"Look here, you girls," he blurted out at last. "You know that Criminal?"

"Yes," they said.

"Well, he's in the apple loft."

"No!" they cried. "Gosh!" And they burst into a chorus of excited questions and exclamations.

"Shut up!" yelled Colin. "How can I tell you anything if you all shout like that? Shut up, I tell you!"

They shut up and he related the adventures of the morning.

"But you are sure he *is* the Criminal?" asked Michelle. She was fifteen, and the eldest of the family, and as such always slightly sceptical about the conclusions come to by the younger children.

"Dead certain," said Colin. "The description is the same, and only a soldier could have fought like he did."

"If he's as nice as you say," declared Jacqueline, "we must save him."

"Of course we must," said Colin. "If we don't he'll be hanged."

Colette burst into floods of tears.

"Don't cry, my pet," said Peronelle, the most practical of the family, and the most like her mother. "Peronelle won't let the man be hanged. Leave it all to me. I shall have one of my inspirations."

A gong sounded, and Colette's tears ceased as though a tap had been turned off.

"Dinner," she said, and led the way indoors.

They ate boiled cod in silence, but the spotted dog, full of currants and with brown sugar on the top, loosened their tongues.

"Couldn't the Criminal have some?" asked Colette with her mouth full. She was unselfish and liked to share her beautiful food with others, and as they had crossed the courtyard they had heard a bellowing noise from the loft that had seemed to her suggestive of hunger.

"Better not," said Colin. "Better not go to him till we've got some plan. . . . He's got the apples. . . . Have you thought of anything yet, 'Nelle?"

"There's only one thing to be done," said Peronelle. "Disguise him and keep him here as one of our relations. There's a beard in the acting box." She was interrupted by the sudden entrance of Toinette. "Go away, Toinette!" she cried indignantly. "We haven't even begun our second helpings!"

But Toinette clung to the door handle, her eyes nearly falling out of her head. "The police!" she gasped. "Outside in the lane, asking for M'sieur du Frocq!"

The children sprang to their feet as one child.

"Now leave it to me," said Peronelle.

With the others trooping behind her she led the way out to the old doorway beneath its massive stone lintel. Outside in the lane stood two large policemen, Guilbert Laroche and Frank Portier, with behind them a handful of young hooligans from the village at Breton Bay, augmented by the Bon Repos milkman, Matthieu Torode, and Jean Lihou, the cats' meat man.

"Father's out," said Peronelle firmly. "What do you want?"

"It's like this, Mamselle," explained Laroche apologetically. "This here Criminal. He's been seen in these parts."

"*We* haven't seen him," said Peronelle haughtily.

"No, Mamselle," said Laroche. "But if you'd just allow us to come and look round the farm. He might be in hiding in one of your outhouses and you none the wiser."

"Certainly not!" said Peronelle, her amber eyes, that were like a tiger's when she was angry, flashing stormily.

"We shan't cause you any inconvenience, Mamselle," Portier assured her meekly. . . . He was a timid man, and Peronelle in a rage was enough to make even a policeman tremble.

"We allow no one to come in here when our father and mother are out," Peronelle assured him. "Good afternoon."

Laroche began to grow a little truculent. "Now look here, you youngsters," he began, but he was not allowed to continue, for Colin, suddenly seizing the generalship of the affair away from Peronelle, was issuing orders at the top of his voice. . . . He had remembered those old days when Bon Repos had been a fortress.

"Defend the gate!" he yelled. "Colette, lock the garden door! Jacqueline, bring out chairs for a barricade! Michelle and Peronelle, stand by me!"

It was a grand fight, the second grand fight of that eventful day. The two policemen made valiant attempts to restore order but were permitted to do no such thing by the hooligans of Breton Bay and Bon Repos. Jacqueline and Colette, dashing backward and forward from house to gate, brought out all the portable parlour furniture they could lay their hands on to form a barricade, Matthieu, the milkman, realizing after only a second's thought where his loyalty lay, leaped to the help of the gallant defenders while Jean Lihou, the cats' meat man, backed the invaders.

They fought gloriously for ten minutes, kicking, pummelling, cheering, shouting, and there is no knowing what might not have happened had not the ears of the invaders, during a lull when they paused to take breath, caught a growing tumult of sound from somewhere across the courtyard.

"Hi!" yelled a hooligan. "There's a man shut in that loft!"

There was no doubt about it. Behind the door at the top of the steps that idiot of a Criminal was idiotically drawing attention to his whereabouts by kicking the door and shouting with the full force of an immensely powerful pair of lungs. . . . Was the man mad?

Pausing to ask themselves this question the children were momentarily off their guard. The hooligans saw it and attacked again. In a final glorious charge, battle cries rending the air and fists whirling like mad, they surged in over the wreck of Rachell's parlour furniture, stampeded across the courtyard and up the steps to the door of the loft, Laroche and Portier lolloping after and the children bringing up the rear.

"They won't get in!" whispered Colin to the weeping girls, wiping a bloody nose on his sleeve. "I'll die before I give up the key!"

But, alas, the loft door was old and the lock was weak. Before the onslaught of half a dozen strong young shoulders it heaved, cracked, and gave way, and the whole crowd of them went tumbling in head over heels like a river in spate.

"I couldn't help it!" wailed Colin heartbrokenly to his Pirate-Criminal. "Oh, I couldn't help it!"

The behaviour of the Criminal in this awful hour seemed to the children absolutely superb. He showed no smallest trace of fear. He stood there before them all, drawn to his full height, with his splendid leonine head thrown back and his eyes blazing. At first he was so angry that, though his throat worked, he could not speak; then words came with a sort of deep-sea roar that cowed the whole crowd to silence.

"What's the time?"

"Half-past two, M'sieur," quavered a weak little voice that was traced to the cats' meat man.

"Ye gods!" cried the Criminal. "And the Luncheon was to have been at one!" He strode forward, scattering the crowd with vigorous shoves to right and left. "Three miles to town! Get me a carriage, somebody! Or a horse! An omnibus! A moving van! Anything!" And he raced down the steps like the wind.

"Why didn't you catch him?" gasped Peronelle to the bewildered Laroche.

"It's not him, Mamselle."

"Then who is it?"

"M'sieur Falaise," said Laroche disgustedly. "And I'd be glad if you'd explain to your Ma, Mamselle, that it ain't the fault of the police if her furniture's smashed to matchwood."

But Peronelle was paying no attention to him. In a flash she was down the steps and across the courtyard, catching up with the Angered Actor at the gate.

"Matthieu's milk-cart!" she yelled. "It goes like the wind! Quick! Quick!"

The conveyance in question was standing in the lane, with Mathilde, its piebald horse, peacefully enjoying a meal of the luscious green grass beneath the hedge. With one agile leap the Actor was inside it, with the five children scrambling in after him.

"The milk-cans!" they shouted. "Throw out the cargo! Lighten the ship!"

The Island milk-cans, beautiful balloon-shaped things that are found nowhere else in the world, came spinning out of the cart almost into the face of the outraged Matthieu, the Actor gathered up the reins, cracked the whip over Mathilde's back, and they were off like a whirlwind, leaving the police, the hooligans, Matthieu, and the cats' meat man staring stupidly after them from the wreck of Rachell's parlour furniture.

How describe the exhilaration of that drive? A moment's thought will convince anyone that a milk-cart is the direct descendant of the Roman chariot, and to watch a high-spirited milkman hurrying home to lunch is almost to hear the cheers that arose in the

Great Circus of Imperial Rome when the winner thundered in to victory. But strangely enough the ancestry of the Bon Repos milk-cart had not been apparent to the children until this moment when, breathless and speechless, their hair streaming in the wind and their internal organs playing leapfrog inside them, they clung to the sides of the cart and prayed to the gods to preserve them from sudden death. The familiar landscape seemed streaming by on the wind of their going; trees and low stone cottages, flower-filled gardens and fragrant hedgerows disappeared almost as quickly as seen. They blinked and they gasped, and every now and then they glanced with fear and admiration at the figure of the man towering above them.

Rupert Falaise played many parts that day, but perhaps the one that showed him to best advantage was that of the Charging Charioteer. He stood upright, superbly balanced, his feet wide apart and his knees slightly bent to take the motion of the chariot. He held the reins skilfully in his left hand, and with his right he kept his whiplash coiling serpent-like over Mathilde's broad back, not whipping her but cajoling her into speed. Now and then he spoke to her, coaxing her softly, and now and then, for sheer joy of the race, he flung back his head and laughed.

But it was a long time before the children could laugh. It was not until Mathilde, who though a fine goer was after all a mortal horse and no Pegasus, began to tire and the speed slackened that they could even recover speech, and it was not until they reached the town of Saint Pierre, with its steep, narrow cobbled streets where the chariot had to go sedately and with care, that they became anything like themselves.

"Well!" they said. "Gosh!"

"Wouldn't he be splendid as the Charioteer in father's play?" said Colin.

"He was jolly nearly a Murderer after all," said Peronelle.

"I thought my last hour had come," said Michelle.

"I felt sick," said Jacqueline.

"And we never had our second helpings of spotted dog!" mourned Colette.

"Did I ask you young demons to come with me?" demanded the Charioteer.

"It's our milk-cart," they pointed out. "It was very kind of us to lend it to you."

"I dare say," said the Charioteer grimly. "But I should like to point out that you owe me a good deal more than the loan of a milk-cart for messing up my engagements in the way you have. Why on earth did you leave me all that time in that damn loft?"

"We meant well," they said. "It was all done out of kindness. We thought you were the man who murdered the Sergeant. We were going to help you to escape. We didn't want you to be hanged. We defended you with our life's blood and all the parlour furniture."

The Charioteer at last saw light. . . . He laughed and laughed.

"Sporting little beasts," he conceded. "But who told you the Sergeant was murdered?"

"Toinette, our maid."

"Well, he isn't. He was only stunned. The poor fool who attacked him will only be had up for assault, and he'll get off lightly, they say."

"Oh!" they said. "Oh! Now everything's lovely again!" And they too laughed and laughed.

If the Luncheon was a failure, owing to the inexplicable absence of the guest of honour, the Reception was a howling success. It is true that the sudden entrance of the Gifted Guest, clad in a blue shirt and flannel trousers stained with sea water, and accompanied by five children with bloodied noses, blackened eyes, and torn garments, was a bit of a shock to the well-dressed assembly gathered in the Guildhall, but when, in a charming speech made from the platform, the situation was explained by the gifted one, the shock changed to riotous enjoyment. . . . Never had a civic ceremony been attended by so much mirth. . . . The only people who did not altogether enjoy themselves were André and Rachell, who once again, as so often before, found themselves the centre of attraction as the parents of the five most disreputable children on the Island.

Yet Rachell had her wish, for an introduction to Rupert Falaise was attained with the minimum of difficulty.

"Where are you staying?" she asked him when everything was at last over.

"I have rooms at Breton Bay, Madame."

"Then Bon Repos is almost on your way home. Come back with us and have a good meal. . . . You

look tired," she added, with a melting, cooing mother-
liness that was irresistible.

"It *has* been a tiring day," Rupert admitted. "But
I have no doubt, Madame, that I shall count it one of
the most fortunate days of my life."

There could be no doubt as to his meaning, for he
glanced appreciatively at each du Frocq in turn, his
eyes resting longest upon Rachell herself and that little
brown rascal Colin. . . . He was once more a Captive.
. . . As she swept out of the Guildhall upon his arm
Rachell could already hear the thunder of applause
that would greet the final descent of the curtain upon
André's play, for she knew without the shadow of a
doubt that they had captured a Family Friend of
Immense Influence.

They drove quietly home in the cool of the evening,
André and Rachell and the elder girls going first in the
carriage and Rupert with Colin and Colette following
behind in the milk-cart. The wind had dropped, and
the cool deep lanes, where the wild roses were in bud
and little streams ran tinkling along beneath green
hart's-tongue ferns, seemed leading them further and
further down into the heart of peace. All the way
home they could hear the murmur of the sea. Now
and then, through a break in a tall hedge, they could
see it. The mermaids had driven the white horses
home to their stables under the cliffs, and the sea was
as pale and smooth and opal-tinted as the sky above
it. There was not a cloud in the sky or a whisper of
wind in the tree tops. Dark purple shadows were

spread behind bushes and walls, hiding places for the Island goblins, the sarregousets, and over each farm-yard pond was spread a green carpet of weed for the dancing feet of the water fairies.

"What a day!" muttered Rupert. "What a country for make-believe! Is it any wonder we Islanders never grow up?"

Chapter Two

THE WELL OF SAINT GEORGE

"Humph!" said Grandpapa, straightening himself, "quite a nasty little feverish attack. Probably brought on by overeating."

"Nonsense, Father!" flashed Rachell, eyeing her father-in-law with disfavour. "Jacqueline never over-eats! It's true we had the first gooseberry tart of the season yesterday, but she only had one quite small helping of it. She's never a greedy child."

Jacqueline, conscious of having seen the remains of the tart going to waste in the larder and having finished it at a sitting from motives of economy only, did not contradict her mother but moved her small dark head restlessly on the pillow and sobbed. To-morrow was her best friend Julie de Putron's birthday party and it was the dearest wish of her heart to be present at it. Her heart had at the moment no other wish in the whole world. Her wish would not be granted, of course, nothing she longed for was ever hers. Every cup of joy to which she stretched out her hand was always immediately withdrawn. Everything always went wrong with her. Everything. She was born unfortunate. She was born misunderstood. She sobbed again.

"She *must* be well by to-morrow, Grandpapa," announced Peronelle, standing beside her mother facing him where he stood upon the other side of Jacqueline's bed. "She's going to Julie de Putron's birthday party."

"She's doing nothing of the sort," snorted Grandpapa. "Birthday party? What? What? What does a birthday party matter compared to health? She's staying comfortably in bed taking the medicine prescribed by her old Grandpapa, and maybe that temperature will go down in a day or two, or maybe it won't, but in any case she won't be up till the end of the week at earliest. These things have to run their course. Nasty affairs, these spring feverish attacks, especially when the result of acute digestive disturbance."

"Digestive my hat!" exploded Peronelle, flying suddenly into one of her hot tempers and tossing back her golden curls as a lion his mane. "That's what you always say. As a matter of fact, Grandpapa, I don't believe you have any idea what's the matter with her. Nor what to do about it. And what's the use of your being a doctor if you can't get her well in time for Julie's party to-morrow? I don't know what one calls doctors in for, I don't really. They very seldom do anything, but if they do do anything what they do do is bound to be wrong. Look at that time I came out in spots, and you said it was stomachic and gave me gregory powder, and then it wasn't stomachic, it was chicken-pox—which I'd said it was all along, only you wouldn't listen—and then by the time you'd found out it wasn't stomachic but chicken-pox I'd given it to every one at school. . . . But then of course you attended every

38

one at school, and they all adored you and thought you a marvellous doctor. . . . And I didn't give you away, of course. I always think one shouldn't give away one's relations, even though of course one can't help seeing through them sometimes, and so I said at the time to Mother that——"

"That will do, Peronelle," thundered Rachell, while Grandpapa on the other side of the bed flung back his splendid old head and gave forth a roar of such fury that it positively shook the room.

"What? What? A nice set of grandchildren you've given me," he bellowed at Rachell. "Here's one of 'em in bed as a result of over-indulgence in gooseberry tart—which I've said time and again should not be taken by those of tender years, but never a word I say is attended to by anyone in this house—and another of 'em insulting me by the bedside of my own patient in a manner that I should not tolerate for a single moment were it not that I—er—that—er—what? What?"

He paused, for Rachell had dissolved into fits of soft laughter. "You and Peronelle!" she gasped, feeling for her handkerchief. "You're so exactly alike sometimes! The way you fling back your heads when you're in rages, the way you always know best, your eloquence, your—— Oh dear! Oh dear! Married to the du Frocqs one is at least never dull!" And propped against the bed-post she wiped tears of mirth from her eyes.

Grandpapa gazed at his daughter-in-law coldly, then looked across the bed at Peronelle. Their bright hazel eyes, identical in shape and colour, met with sudden sympathy. This woman who has married into our family, they said to each other wordlessly, this beloved but incomprehensible woman, her sense of humour is not ours. But then, poor thing, she was not originally a du Frocq. One must make allowances.

"Mother!" reproached Peronelle in dulcet tones. "I don't think all this noise can be good for Jacqueline. Take Grandpapa downstairs to write out that prescription. I'll see to Jacqueline."

"Come along, Grandpapa dear," said Rachell gently, drawing herself up to her full lovely height and slipping her handkerchief into her waistband beside the bunch of primroses that she wore there. "We'll do what Peronelle says. We always do what Peronelle says in this family." And she led the way superbly towards the door, restraining herself with some difficulty from pointing out that whoever it was who had made a row it had not been Rachell du Frocq. She was used to exercising restraints of this sort, and had indeed elevated self-control to such a fine art that a family of seven impulsive hot-tempered people owed it to her, and her alone, that they lived together in one small farmhouse in a state of inviolable happiness. . . . A wonderful woman. . . . Grandpapa followed her to the door with a deference that was no less a tribute to her powers because it was quite unconsciously paid.

Peronelle was left looking pitifully down at her younger sister, her brow wrinkled in thought and one finger laid professionally upon Jacqueline's pulse. For in spite of her diatribe against doctors Peronelle was firmly determined to be one when she grew up. The medical profession needed setting to rights, she thought. . . . Besides, doctoring was in her blood.

"How do you feel now?" she asked Jacqueline.

"Awful," whispered Jacqueline, two tears squeezing themselves out from under her shut eyelids. "It's my tummy."

"It's my belief you've got internal gout," said Peronelle. "Like Aunt Sophie had."

"Grandpapa said not," murmured Jacqueline. "I suggested that but he just pooh-poohed. Oh, 'Nelle, I *did* want to go to that party!" And rolling over she buried her face in her pillow and sobbed as though her heart was breaking.

"Jackie, darling, you shall!" cried Peronelle, flinging herself down upon the bed beside her little sister, her arm round her neck and her cheek pressed against hers. "You *shall*. 'Nelle will see to it all. 'Nelle will make you all well again."

"You don't know how," moaned Jacqueline. "Grandpapa can't, and he's a doctor."

"He doesn't understand your case, darling," Peronelle explained loftily. "Now I do. It's not gooseberries, it's gout. I've read about gout and everything seems to me to point to it. We must give you something to reduce the inflammation, darling, and then you will be well. We must apply something."

"What?" asked Jacqueline.

"I haven't decided yet," said Peronelle. "I am just turning over various alternative treatments in my mind. But don't you worry, my pet. I shall have one of my inspirations. Bound to. Don't you worry."

Jacqueline sighed and nestled closer. She had unbounded trust in Peronelle. Everyone had. Peronelle's faith in her own powers was of the sort that moves mountains, and in the course of family history mountains had not infrequently been moved by it. Jacqueline sighed again, a fluttering trustful sigh.

"That's right, duckie," cooed Peronelle, perceiving that the seed of faith had been sown. "You cuddle up and go to sleep and presently I'll be back with something to make you well. I promise."

She kissed Jacqueline, pulled the bedclothes more firmly round her, and stole softly downstairs past the parlour door where Grandpapa was still booming away to Rachell about early gooseberries, through the kitchen and out to the back door porch, where Colette, the baby of the family, was sitting weeping for Jacqueline with so much water and so much noise that Toinette their maidservant was keeping her distance, lest she be not only drowned but deafened.

"Oh, don't let her die, 'Nelle!" roared Colette. "Don't let her die!"

"Of course she's not going to die!" shouted Peronelle above the din. "Don't cry, my pet. 'Nelle will make Jackie well again."

But though she spoke with decision, and sitting down on the door-sill lifted Colette to her lap with a most confident gesture, she was not in reality quite so much in command of the situation as she would have liked

42

to be. . . . What *did* one apply for gout? . . . She
looked out over the garden, biting her little finger,
mutely asking the glorious spring world about her for
help in the solving of this problem.

It was as yet inarticulate, but in its loveliness there
was promise. Spring was always heavenly in the
Channel Islands, but this year it was even more
heavenly than usual. Over her head the new leaves of
the lilac trees were like green flames. During the
pauses between Colette's outbursts of lamentation she
could hear the shouting of the birds and the song of
the wind as it raced in from the sea. The trees, tossing
against the bright blue of the sky, were rosy with the
crowding buds, and primroses were scattered in every
sheltered hollow. . . . It was iniquitous that Jacqueline
should be ill in weather like this.

"What *can* I do?" demanded Peronelle aloud
of the kitchen garden.

At this moment Toinette, Colette having quieted
down, ventured to appear at the back door to shake
out the mats. "Go to old M'dame Dumaresq, Mamselle," she advised in her pretty broken English. "She
is wise, is old M'dame Dumaresq. She say that the
cure for all illness is in the earth. She say there is
nothing she cannot cure with the 'erbs in 'er garden.
She cured my grandfather Matthieu Mauger of fits with
a good dose of rosmarin and marjolaine boiled in 'oly
water, and a good beating about the shoulders with 'er
stick. 'E 'ad a devil in 'im, so she say, and the rosmarin and marjolaine uprooted the devil from 'is
stomach, while the beating assisted of it out. Terrible

43

were the fits of my grandfather; 'e would shout at us and throw 'is boots at our 'eads till we yelled for mercy. But M'dame Dumaresq cured 'im. 'E was frightened of 'er stick."

"All superstition," pronounced Peronelle, who went to a High School and was enlightened. "Rosemary and marjoram couldn't possibly cure fits, and there are no devils nowadays, they went out of fashion years and years ago."

"All illness is of the devil, Mamselle," pronounced Toinette. "The devil 'e may be out of fashion, but 'e is still with us. But yes, very much with us." She shook out another mat, and snorted with contempt for Peronelle's point of view. "The poor Mamselle Jacqueline! Monsieur le docteur pronounce 'imself incapable of curing 'er in time for 'er party, and 'er sisters they will not put themselves to the trouble of walking down to the cottage of M'dame Dumaresq to procure the 'ealing of 'er 'erbs."

"How dare you, Toinette!" cried Peronelle, leaping to her feet in a rage. "Not put myself to the trouble? You know very well, Toinette Henriette Dubois, that I am ready at any moment to cut myself into small snippets for my family. Who said I wasn't going to the wise woman? *I* didn't say so. As a matter of fact I am going at once. Though I naturally do not hold with country superstition I am well aware that amongst its accretions there is frequently a certain modicum of common sense."

"*Mon Dieu!*" gasped Toinette, but though she found the meaning of this lofty High School language not altogether clear Peronelle's purpose was quite plain, for her slim figure was already lost to sight among the currant bushes as she raced towards the garden gate.

"Me too!" yelled Colette, trundling after. "Me too, 'Nelle!"

"Come on, then," called Peronelle. "Run, duckie, run!"

Toinette, gathering up her mats, departed triumphantly indoors. Mamselle Peronelle was not one to put her hand to the plough and then turn back. M'dame Dumaresq would now certainly be visited, and the last ounce of her wisdom extracted from her. Mamselle Jacqueline's recovery was now, Toinette thought, as good as accomplished.

The lane led past the courtyard in front of the house and here Rachell, who had just seen off Grandpapa, was lingering a moment to feed her doves.

"Where are you going?" she demanded in surprise, as Peronelle and Colette ran by.

"For a walk," they said, passing hastily on lest any awkward questions should be asked.

"Don't go too far," called Rachell, and stepped out into the lane to watch them out of sight. They looked rather enchanting, she thought. Peronelle's twinkling bare legs and golden head gleamed in the sun as though they had been polished; while little Colette, fair and fat and cherubic in a scarlet jersey, was as satisfying a sight as could be seen upon an April morning. They had both outgrown the jerseys they wore, and though their skirts had originally been designed to hide their knees they were now totally inadequate for their original purpose. Yet this suggestion of bursting out and shooting upwards was not unattractive; it was all in keeping with the spring; and the children themselves might have been the light and warmth and growth of spring made visible in human form.

They swerved to their right along a sandy lane that wound between high grassy banks crowned with the stunted Island oak trees, that stretched their twisted wind-blown branches high overhead to make an inter-laced ceiling for the little lane. The leaves on the oak trees were still only half unfurled, crinkly and coral-tipped, and through them the sun shone in long golden shafts that lit like pointing fingers upon the primroses and bright green ferns growing in the banks. There was a magic in the morning that made Peronelle's golden curls quiver round her face as though each one was alive and dancing, and made Colette chirrup and crow and bowl along at a most unusual pace. On such a day, thought Peronelle, drawing great breaths of the primrose-scented air, old tales should live again and the giants and saints of old time once more stalk the world in power and beauty. She could see them in her mind's eye, arrogant in their immortality, flowers springing from the print of their feet and wells of water from the green dells where they stopped to rest.

And just at that moment they turned the corner by St. George's well. The green bank swung back in a semicircle enclosing a little grassy hollow where a spring bubbled up from beneath a flat stone, spread into a round clear pool fringed by forget-me-nots and then ran away downhill towards the sea, tinkling merrily over the pebbles but almost hidden from sight beneath hart's-tongue ferns that bent over it to protect it from too inquisitive eyes. . . . For this was a holy well. . . . Behind the spring, beneath the canopy of oak leaves, was an old grey stone of incredible age rudely fashioned into the shape of a cross. St. George had put it there, so said the peasants, when centuries ago he had visited the Island in company with St. Patrick, both saints worn out by their labours for the savage and ungrateful people of England and Ireland, and in search of a little relaxation and amusement in a less exacting neighbourhood. They found them on the Island, and so grateful were they that St. George caused a spring to gush out of the earth in his favourite dell, while St. Patrick obligingly gathered up all the toads, snakes and noxious creatures he could find, stuffed them into his wallet and carried them off to be let loose at some future date, as he should see fit, upon some inferior and less amusing island.

Many were the stories told of this well. The nicest one told how a little boy left his canary's cage open, and the bird flew away towards the well, the little boy running after it in such hot pursuit that he would have fallen in and been drowned had not the neighing of a horse made him stop and look round, to see the fiery head of St. George's charger disappearing among the oak trees; and his canary sitting on top of the cross singing loudly. The peasants said that ever since that day, when St. George had saved a child from death, the water of the well was a certain cure for all diseases, especially the diseases of children, and they told tales of the miraculous cures that had taken place; all equally picturesque and unlikely, but yet, on a morning such as this, they claimed a passing thought, and made Peronelle and Colette pause a moment at the well, watching the shadows of the leaves caressing the old grey cross and listening to the gurgling of the water as it welled up under the flat stone.

"Nice man," cooed Colette, referring, apparently, to St. George.

"I like St. Patrick best," said Peronelle. "I *hate* toads."

They went on down the lane, which narrowed until it became a stony path running down the cliff, clamorous with the gurgling of the stream, which became more and more excited as it drew nearer to the sea, and with the shouting of the birds in the trees above their heads. The trees thinned, so that they could see chunks of blue sea and sky through the pattern of the leaves, and finally ended altogether as the path ran out on a flat, rock-sheltered plateau at the edge of the cliff.

And here, built of the same grey rock that sheltered it, with a thatched roof held in place against winter storms by wire netting weighted with heavy stones, was Madame Dumaresq's cottage. In a sheltered patch of ground behind it was her garden, full to overflowing with flowers and herbs, and in front of it, seated upon a low stone wall backed with tamarisk trees and fuchsia bushes, were her six black cats.

The children paused a moment, for the cats looked

large and fierce, and it is well known on the Island—
though of course Peronelle didn't believe it—that
black cats are in league with the devil himself.

"They won't hurt us," she said stoutly, remembering she was a High School girl. "Nice pussies! Nice,
good pussies!"

"Nice pussies!" chirruped Colette courageously,
from a place of complete safety behind her sister.

The cats arose and looked at them, tails twitching,
green eyes fixed upon the children in a rude and un-
blinking stare. However, the conclusions come to were
apparently favourable, for they narrowed their eyes in
condescending tolerance, leaped off the wall and led
the way up the path to the cottage door, where they sat
back on their haunches with expectant eyes fixed upon
the door latch.

Peronelle knocked. "Enter," said a shrill, quavering old voice, and they lifted the latch and walked in,
preceded by the cats in single file and greeted by the
friendly sound that so often meets visitors at an
Island cottage, the tap-tap of bobbins upon a lace
pillow.

Seated by the fire, with her lace pillow upon her lap,
was the tiniest, cleanest, merriest old woman Peronelle
and Colette had ever set eyes upon. She was hardly
bigger than a child, and bent almost double by the
weight of her years. Her face was as brown and
wrinkled as a walnut and her chin and nose almost met
each other, but out of this mask of age peered dark eyes
as gay and bright as a child's. She wore an old black
skirt that with age had taken on the green sheen of a

cock's feather, a snowy white apron over it, a scarlet shawl folded across her chest, and a white frilled cap that entirely hid her hair and was tied beneath her chin in a very demure bow. All old ladies should wear a white cap, thought Peronelle, for it makes them look so good; the whole attraction of old age to the young lies in its air of saintliness achieved after long struggle. There was no knowing whether Madame Dumaresq was a saint or not—in fact on close inspection of her mischievous face one might have guessed not—but with those snowy nun-like folds of starched linen, and that demure bow, she triumphantly looked it.

And so did her room. It was a most austere and attractive room, as clean and tidy as Madame Dumaresq herself. A fire of seaweed burned brightly on the swept hearth and the hard earth floor was spread with clean sand. The oak table and stools, and the carved chest that every peasant bride takes to her home to hold her dower of bridal linen, were dark and shiny with age and much polishing, the small Island milk-cans that hung upon the wall, delightful things shaped like blown balloons, sparkled like silver, and the dried fern that covered the *jonquiere* or "green bed" smelled so sweet when Peronelle sat upon it that she knew it had been growing on the cliff not long ago. The whole place inspired her with such glowing confidence that she plunged at once into an eager description of Jacqueline's symptoms and predicament.

"You see, Madame," she cried, "you see how important it is that Jacqueline should go to Julie's party. Julie is her best friend and only last week they pricked

"ENTER," SAID A SHRILL, QUAVERING OLD VOICE

their fingers and mingled the blood and vowed eternal friendship."

"And poor Jacqueline has a pain in her tummy," cried Colette pitifully, laying her own plump hands upon the part affected. "It is drefful wicked that Jacqueline should have a pain!" And two fat tears overflowed and rolled lugubriously off her rounded cheeks upon the sanded floor.

"But yes, my children," said Madame Dumaresq, shaking her old head with deep solemnity. "I fully understand the wickedness of it. I fully understand, too, the importance of the party given by Mamselle Julie. The little Jacqueline must certainly be cured, and that instantly."

"You think you can cure her?" asked Peronelle eagerly.

"But yes, my pretty ones," smiled Madame with supreme confidence. "It is a very common affliction, this that you have described to me. A dose of la campana for her little inside, and for outside an application of violet leaves boiled in holy water, will work an instant cure. This indisposition of the little Jacqueline is one that is very prevalent with young things when the moon is at the full, and is caused primarily by the spring tides."

"But not caused by overeating," announced Peronelle belligerently.

"*Pas certainement!*" cried Madame in powerful indignation. "Little girls never overeat! It is only little boys who are sometimes tempted to a slight indiscretion, and for them I prescribe l'alliene, the wormwood, a very nasty medicine that would be unsuitable for delicate female organs. La campana is a gentle herb, a holy herb used by the Druids of old, a sweet-tasting medicine agreeable to those of extreme sensibility."

"Jacqueline *does* suffer from extreme sensibility," said Peronelle eagerly. "She always cries a lot when she has a pain, and she won't take nasty medicines— she tips them out of window. That's why Grandpapa can never do her any good, because all his medicines are always nasty."

"La campana, *mes enfants*, is delicious," Madame assured them.

Peronelle looked at her with glowing admiration. Now *here* was a proper doctor. No insulting nonsense about overeating, no perhaps this and perhaps the other, no nasty medicine, but instant promise of a complete cure and assurance that there would be no unpleasantness in the course of it. She understood, did Madame Dumaresq, that you paid a doctor to *cure* you, not to come dithering round saying a thing must run its course, which goodness knew it would do anyhow without your having to pay him to come and say so. She wished Grandpapa would take a lesson in professional behaviour from Madame Dumaresq, she did indeed. That Madame would cure Jacqueline she had not now a single doubt, and neither had Colette, and when Madame got to her feet and took down a milk-can from the wall, and her stick from a corner, they both leaped up eagerly, prepared to follow her to the death.

But they only had to follow her up the lane to dip

some holy water out of the stream. It was fun to part the ferns and plunge the bright little can into the sparkline ice-cold water. Colette laughed while she did it, and when she had handed the can to Peronelle she held up her fat fingers starfish-wise against the sun and chirruped to see the wet drops running down them like flashing diamonds.

"Jewels," crooned old Madame Dumaresq, peering at them. "The jewels of St. George. Have you ever heard this saying, *mes petits choux*?

> Good Saint George who slew the dragon,
> Slay the evil that besets me.
> Slay the aches that curse my stomach,
> Slay the sins that cloud my spirit.
> Shield my head from storms and tempests,
> Shield my feet from slips and tumbles.
> Good Saint George, a child prays to you,
> Guard me as you guard all children.

It is very efficacious, and should be repeated when the violet leaves are applied to the little Jacqueline."

In her back garden, while they picked the violet leaves and laid them in a little basket of plaited grass, Madame showed the children all the herbs and plants that, in conjunction with the holy water, were for the healing of the ills of mankind. "There was never yet a disease upon this earth, my dears," she said, "but out of the earth there did not grow the cure for it." And pointing with her stick she rattled off the names of her precious plants.

There were masses of them in her garden. The violet leaves themselves, unrivalled as a poultice, la cassidone the French lavender whose flowers and leaves cause saliva to flow again in dried-up mouths, la rue which cures blindness, l'alliene, or wormwood, so excellent for overeating, la petite sauche the small-leaved sage, le grand consoul, la marjolaine, la campana the holy herb of the Druids, and many others that Madame Dumaresq found equally effective. "But," she said, "while they are being planted he who plants must swear a little. Not blasphemously, of course, my dears, but in a genteel fashion, using such oaths as 'goderabetin' and 'godzamin'. It is so that the Evil Eye is averted. I do not know why. I only know that it is so."

"Would it be a good thing to swear while we dose Jacqueline?" Peronelle asked earnestly.

"It might be as well, my dears," said Madame Dumaresq, and Colette, lest she should forget the important words, murmured over and over again in a hoarse whisper: "Goderabetin, Godzamin, Goderabetin, Godzamin."

Then they went indoors, and Madame Dumaresq, with her back carefully turned to the children, took a bottle of medicine out of the cupboard beside her fireplace, changed the label on it, which said very clearly in large capitals, "L'ALLIENE," for another which said in equally large capitals, "LA CAMPANA," wrapped it up in a cool fresh dock leaf and handed it to Peronelle. "There you are, my dear," she said. "Let her drink half the bottle early this afternoon and the other half an hour or so later. And as soon as possible boil the violet leaves and apply them externally as hot as possible. You understand, *mes enfants*? La campana *inside* and the violet leaves *outside*. There must be no confusion. I have known cases where there was confusion, the external remedy being applied internally and the internal one externally, and the results in these cases were not entirely satisfactory. Come back in the morning, my dears, that you may return to me my milk-can and my basket."

"Yes," said Peronelle, "and tell you how Jacqueline is."

"There will be no necessity for that," said Madame Dumaresq confidently. "The little Jacqueline is as good as cured already."

Peronelle stood up, clasping the milk-can and the medicine bottle and handing the basket of violet leaves to Colette. Then she faced Madame Dumaresq, flushing a bright pink. "Your—your—the doctor's fee," she murmured. "It may have to wait until I have saved up a little more pocket money, because——"

Madame laughed, and lifting Peronelle's hot face in her hands she kissed it. "There is no fee, *ma petite*," she said. "I would not charge a fee to two such loving little sisters. But if your good mother should want lace to trim your little knickerbockers and your little petticoats, remember that old Suzanne Dumaresq is the best lace-maker on the Island."

Colette, dimpling, lifted her inadequate skirt and gazed at her plain and unadorned blue serge knickerbockers. "Colette would like lots and lots of lace on them," she cooed.

The Well of Saint George

Madame Dumaresq, laughing, kissed her too, and then went with them to her front door to see them off. "Sweet little cabbages!" she murmured. "Stop at the well and thank the good God for life and love and laughter."

"*There's* a doctor for you!" said Peronelle to Colette as they ran off. "Why, she hasn't even *charged* us anything! That's what I call being a really nice doctor!"

They were back late, with only just time to hide the milk-can, medicine bottle and basket in the lilac bush by the back door before the bell rang peremptorily for dinner.

Over the boiled cod Rachell said sadly that Jacqueline was not so well. She had cried herself sick and though Grandpapa had sent up a bottle of medicine at once it hadn't so far seemed to do her any good. She hadn't liked the taste of it and had been naughty about taking it. "I shall have to stay at home this afternoon and see that she *does* take it," sighed Rachell. "I shan't be able to go into town with you, André."

Her husband sighed, and laid down an untasted piece of cod with an air of dejection. He and Rachell had planned this little shopping expedition together weeks ago. They were so busy, he with the farm and she with the children, that they seldom could do anything together, and on the rare occasions when they did think they had achieved a half-holiday it was always wrested from them. . . . Well, it couldn't be helped. . . . He lifted the cod again, ate it, and sighed in increasing dejection, for Toinette's cooking, always of the watery type, was in this hour of crisis even more sloppy than usual.

Peronelle, noticing her father's depression, hastened to the rescue. "Poor father!" she said. "It's a shame he shouldn't have his outing. Leave it all to me, Mother. *I'll* see to it. I'm quite good at the children and their medicine."

"Yes, darling, you are," said her mother with admiration. Peronelle was indeed an excellent disciplinarian. She combined a real and sympathetic knowledge of what other people ought to do with so iron a determination that they should do it that they immediately did do it. "You're splendid, darling. I think I might perhaps leave Jacqueline to you. It's just a case of keeping her warm and covered up and giving the medicine. I'll explain to you later. What, Colette? *Another* apple dumpling? You mustn't overeat, sweetheart, or you'll be ill like poor Jacqueline."

"Little girls," said Colette, "never overeat."

"There," said Peronelle, hanging out of Jacqueline's bedroom window and listening to the sounds of departing carriage wheels, "they've gone. Colette, fetch Madame Dumaresq's medicine and tell Toinette to put the violet leaves on to boil."

Colette scuttled joyously from the room and Peronelle began very carefully to measure out the afternoon dose of Grandpapa's medicine.

"I can't drink it, 'Nelle," moaned Jacqueline. "It's *horrible*. I was sick after I had it this morning. Grandpapa's medicines always make me much, much worse."

"You aren't going to drink it, duckie," Peronelle assured her, and pitched the dose out of the window. "I'm just sparing Mother's feelings. If she came home and found that dose still in the bottle she'd think I wasn't to be trusted, and then she would be grieved. I hate grieving Mother."

"I feel awful, 'Nelle," said Jacqueline. "I think I'm going to die."

"Tommy rot," said Peronelle. "You're going to be cured. Madame Dumaresq promised. In the morning you will be perfectly well. I *know* you will be cured."

Her voice rang out in such triumphant certainty that Jacqueline actually smiled a little, and turned her head eagerly on the pillow when sounds as of a minor earthquake heralded the return of Colette up the stairs.

"The holy water's on the boil," she chirruped, bounding in, "and I've brought my little mug with the robin on it for Jackie to drink her medicine out of. You shall have the mug for your very own, Jackie, for your very own for ever."

Jacqueline sat up with a kindling eye. . . . She had always coveted that robin mug. . . . "Thank you, Colette. You're sure the medicine isn't nasty, 'Nelle?"

"Lovely!" declared Peronelle, pouring it into the robin mug. "It is la campana, grown in Madame Dumaresq's own garden. If you had been a greedy

little boy you would have been given l'alliene, a very
nasty medicine, but Madame never gives nasty medicines
to sensitive little girls. The Druids used la campana,
Jacqueline, in the days when doctors really *were*
doctors, not silly old mugwumps like Grandpapa.
There you are. Drink it down."

Jacqueline took the mug and sipped cautiously,
wrinkling her nose.

"Isn't it good," whispered Peronelle persuasively.
"Can't you taste the flowers growing in Madame's
garden, and the sunshine, and the wind blowing over
the heather from the sea?"

Jacqueline took a large and heartening gulp.

"Do you feel it all nice inside, darlin'?" crooned
Colette. "Do you feel it makin' you all better?"

"Yes," breathed Jacqueline with starry eyes, and
drained the mug to the dregs.

"Godzamin!" shouted Colette suddenly. "Goderabetin! Godzamin! Goderabetin! Godzamin!"

Jacqueline nearly dropped the robin mug.

"It's all right," soothed Peronelle, "that's just to
avert the Evil Eye."

"Was there an Evil Eye?" asked Jacqueline
faintly.

"I don't say there was," said Peronelle. "But *if*
there was *now* there isn't."

But Jacqueline was not quite reassured, and when
sounds as of a major earthquake were heard upon the
stairs she turned a little pale.

"That's not the Evil Eye," soothed Peronelle.
"That's Toinette with the violet leaves."

The Well of Saint George

"You should 'ave seen that 'oly water boil!" panted Toinette, bursting in. "Like diamond jewels, it was, bubbling up so clear and sweet. And when I threw those violet leaves in, believe me or not, Mamselles, that kitchen smelled like Paradise."

"We believe you," said Peronelle solemnly. "This cure is a holy cure, that's why it's so certain. Now slap those leaves down on her tummy, quick, before the heat goes off!"

Colette pulled up the bedclothes, Toinette slapped down the violet leaves upon the affected part and Peronelle pressed the poultice into position and bound it round with her best white silk scarf. "Now, you girls," she whispered impressively, her fingers busy with the green scented leaves, "we won't swear this time. We will keep this an entirely religious ceremony." And she began to chant, Colette accompanying her in the hoarse bass voice that was always hers in moments of excitement.

"Good Saint George who slew the dragon,
Slay the evil that besets me,
Slay the aches that curse my stomach,
Slay the sins that cloud my spirit.
Shield my head from storms and tempests,
Shield my feet from slips and tumbles.
Good Saint George, a child prays to you.
Guard me as you guard all children."

"That's a nice saying," murmured Jacqueline sleepily. "And the leaves feel lovely and warm."

61

"There are more of 'em," whispered Toinette. "And more 'oly water."

"Boil up some more, then," commanded Peronelle. "We'll put on more when these get cold. And then she will go to sleep. And when she wakes up she will be perfectly cured."

"I'm cured *now*," declared Jacqueline.

When Rachell returned it was to find the curtains of Jacqueline's room drawn, Jacqueline fast asleep and Peronelle sitting by her.

"Ssh!" said Peronelle. "She's asleep, and I think she's taken the turn."

"She does look better," whispered Rachell, bending over the bed. Then she straightened herself and picked up Grandpapa's bottle of medicine, which together with a clean medicine glass was standing in a prominent position upon the bedside table. "Two more doses gone now. That's right, Peronelle. Did you have any difficulty, darling, in making her take it?"

"I have had no difficulty about anything," said Peronelle placidly. "I told you before that I'm quite good with the children and their medicine."

"You're wonderful, darling," said Rachell, and having kissed the two rosy faces, one flushed with triumph and the other with returning health, she withdrew to take off her bonnet in the humblest possible frame of mind.

"Can't understand it," said Grandpapa next morning. "No fever. No pain. Looks as fit as a fiddle."

Jacqueline, dressed and in the best of health, was sitting upon his knee in the parlour. She smiled up at him, dimpling and friendly, for his innocent bewilderment was so touching that it made her feel positively loving towards him. . . . Almost she had forgiven him that vile medicine that had made her sick.

"It was your medicine, Grandpapa," said Rachell gently. "I always say your medicines are wonderful."

Peronelle, standing by with Colette, smiled radiantly at Grandpapa. . . . She was remembering a particularly obnoxious bottle of his that she had once poured into the soup.

Grandpapa was touched. "Ah!" he said. "A prophet is without honour in his own country, eh? That's not true of me. What? What? My grandchildren have faith in their old grandfather, eh?" And holding Jacqueline closer with his left arm he stretched out his right to gather in Peronelle and Colette.

Being truthful children they did not answer, they just smiled and smiled like the Cheshire cat. Their consciences did not smite them for they had the satisfaction of knowing that throughout the whole affair they had not told one single lie.

"And I may go to the party?" whispered Jacqueline, her cheek against Grandpapa's.

"She shall!" declared the infatuated old man. "And lest she catch cold she shall go in Grandpapa's very own carriage."

He kissed her, then fearing lest Peronelle and Colette should be jealous kissed them too. What engaging round rosy faces they had, he thought, so trusting and so innocent.

"Dear Grandpapa!" chirruped Colette with genuine affection, and then, "Mother, may we have lace on our new petticoats?"

Rachell laughed. The complete irrelevance of children's remarks always amused her. "If you like, darlings," she said.

"Madame Dumaresq," said Peronelle solemnly, "makes lovely lace."

Chapter Three

RESCUE ON THE ISLAND

ABOVE the harbour the old town of St. Pierre clung to
the steep, rocky hillside as though afraid the storms that
swept over the Island would blow it away altogether.
It was built of grey granite, stained and weather-worn,
and the irregular line of its climbing roofs, with the
steep, twisting gullies of narrow cobbled streets, made
it look more like a pile of rock fretted by wind and
water than a town built by man. On stormy days,
when the grey waves of the English Channel thundered
against the harbour wall and the spray seemed trying
to reach the low racing clouds, the town looked black
and ominous; but on fine days, when ripples of an
unbelievably deep blue lapped softly against the old
grey stone and the clear sky seemed curved over the
Island in the semblance of a crystal dome, the town
too seemed to soften and relax; to catch the reflection
of the sky in pools among the cobbles and the warmth
of the sun in the yellow-lichened roofs.

These were the days that old Jean Garis enjoyed.
The front of his dark little bow-windowed bookshop
looked out on La Rue Lihou, a narrow cobbled street so
steep that climbing it was like climbing the side of a
mountain, but the window of his sitting-room at the

back looked straight out on to the harbour, and when he peeped through the scarlet geraniums that filled it he could see the Islands lying like chunks of uncut opal in the blue water, and beyond them, on clear days, the long, low shape of France.   He was so high up that he seemed to be living on top of a precipice, with the town falling sheer away beneath him to the sea, and when the weather was wild he felt a little afraid and insecure. . . . He did not like the wild days.

For Jean Garis was getting old.   He did not know how old he was, having unfortunately mislaid the family Bible that had inscribed in it the dates of his birth and those of his twelve brothers and sisters, but he thought that he was not far off eighty.   Renouvette Méturier, who kept the sweetshop to his right, was getting old too, though as she was a woman one could not ask how old, and Pierre Duport the chemist, who lived in the shop to the left and had been making his famous verbena scent for fifty years, owned to seventy-five.   Forty years ago La Rue Lihou, in spite of its steepness and narrowness, had been popular with shoppers.   Jean Garis, Renouvette Méturier and Pierre Duport had all been young then. Renouvette's coloured boiled sweets had been the last word in luxury and Jean's shop had been the resort of everyone who gave themselves any intellectual airs at all. . . .   But that had been in the days of sailing ships, when the Island had been almost completely dependent upon local talent. . . .   Things were different now that the nineteenth century was drawing to a close and a steamer arrived daily from England with the newest

IN THE RUE LIHOU

67

confectionery, cosmetics and books for the big new shops at the bottom of the hill behind the harbour; vulgar shops, old Jean Garis thought they were, with their crude paint and polished floors that tripped a man up, and pert assistants, some of them English, who thought they knew everything and in reality knew nothing at all.

Old Jean had known for a long time that the blow was coming, yet when it did actually fall he was as completely bowled over as though he had been unprepared. It fell in the shape of two letters, delivered by hand at lunch time when he was in the middle of a particularly succulent bit of steak, in his little back room looking on the harbour. The first letter was from his lawyer and told him, not for the first time but with a final urgency that got home to him at last, that his shop and stock in trade must be sold at once if he was to avoid the humiliation of bankruptcy; and the second was from his nephew, a farmer on the other side of the Island, and offered him a home for the remainder of his days. . . . It was kind of his nephew, for there was not much love lost between them, and even less between old Jean and the nephew's scolding wife, but the farmer was an upright man who never failed to do his duty with a cold, hard, conscientious thoroughness that made the hearts of those to whom he did it turn to ice within them.

Old Jean could not finish his steak.

He got up and brushed breadcrumbs off the lapels of his black alpaca coat with his clean silk handkerchief, for even in this moment of desolation he remained fastidious. His neatness and comeliness at the age of round-about-eighty were amongst his many attractions, and he knew it and was as proud of his appearance as any girl in her teens. He was thin and dapper, with delicate, blue-veined hands and a face where parchment-coloured skin was stretched tightly over fine bones. He was cleanshaven, and meticulously careful about his daily shave, and the faded blue eyes behind his steel-rimmed spectacles had lost none of their humour and kindliness with the passing of the years. His white hair was still thick and silky everywhere except on top, but as he always wore a black velvet skull-cap to protect the place on top no one but himself knew of the way in which it had let him down.

When he had removed the last crumb he walked slowly to the mantelpiece, his feet dragging a little in a way that annoyed him, and put his two letters behind the black marble clock. They must be answered, of course, and answered soon, but he would not answer them just yet. He would leave himself a few more hours in which to feel that his life and his shop were still his own. . . . Or perhaps, on second thoughts, he would not answer them till to-morrow, and give himself a whole night's respite.

Then he walked to the window and looked out through the scarlet geraniums at the sea and the Islands and the far coast of France. They had been having a week of warm, sunny autumn weather, blue and intensely quiet, the kind of weather that breaks up suddenly in the first of the equinoctial gales and is doubly precious for that reason, but to-day there was a little breeze blowing and the Islands looked ominously clear. Jean mechanically tapped the barometer that hung on the wall beside him and then, in spite of his preoccupation with his troubles, suddenly exclaimed and leaned nearer, peering at it short-sightedly. . . . For it was dropping with considerable speed.

"Something's on the way," murmured old Jean, and wondered if when darkness came it would bring with it one of those wild storms that he dreaded. . . . Only somehow, now, he did not seem to dread them as much as usual. . . . He would rather see out a thousand storms in this little exposed house upon the cliff top than sit secure, a recipient of charity, in his nephew's snug, sheltered farmhouse kitchen. . . . Charity. . . . The beautiful word with its ugly meaning struck him like a blow between the eyes, and for a moment the scarlet of the geraniums seemed to spread like a sheet of flame over the blue and emerald of the Islands and the sea.

The tinkle of the shop bell, that rang automatically when the shop door opened, roused him and he started guiltily and looked at the clock. A quarter past two. The woman who "did" for him was likely to arrive at any moment to wash up and here was he still lingering in the sitting-room when he should have been in the shop. He blew his nose, polished his spectacles, adjusted his black tie and hurried to his duties.

"Good afternoon, M'sieur Garis," said a clear voice from somewhere near the ceiling.

"*Bon jour*, m'sieur," cried another, a yet gayer and clearer voice, from the floor.

Rescue on the Island

Old Jean's strained expression relaxed; he smiled and pushed his spectacles to the top of his head—he had had them many years ago and they were now rather a hindrance than otherwise to clear vision—the better to gaze benevolently at his favourite customers.

They were two girls in their early teens, the daughters of André du Frocq the poet, of whom verse lovers on the Island were inordinately proud, and as such would have been welcome in Jean's bookshop even had he not adored them personally; which he did with the whole strength of his stout old heart. . . . For had they not spent every available moment of their holidays during the last three years amassing knowledge in his shop? And had he not himself guided their reading and superintended the development of their minds? They hardly ever bought anything, but then, dear children, they had no money. Had they been women of wealth he knew that they would have bought every book in the shop. And he never minded if people bought anything; the great thing was that they should love books and use them. His sentiments did him credit, said his lawyer, only unfortunately they were not commercial.

Michelle, the elder, was perched on top of the wooden ladder that Jean used for getting books from the top shelf, reading Aeschylus' *Agamemnon*, in the Greek. She was a thin, lanky, bespectacled girl with straight dark hair strained back from a thin, clever face and confined in a stumpy plait. Long, thin, black-stockinged legs, with the stockings coming down and lying in coils round the ankles, emerged from her skimpy dark-blue skirt and twisted themselves round the ladder.

She smiled absent-mindedly at Jean and went back to *Agamemnon*.

Peronelle, the younger girl, was lying on her front on the floor, her black-stockinged legs kicking in the air, and making a drawing of the human skeleton, with a nasty little pile of bones lying on the floor beside her. . . . She had lately decided to become a lady doctor and Jean had lots of medical books on the bottom shelf. . . . Not even the dark-blue skirt and jersey she had grown out of, or the two tight plaits that stuck out horizontally above her ears and did their best to strain all the curl out of her golden hair, could disguise her beauty. She was like a flame. Her pointed little face, though it was pale, was almost luminous with vitality, and her tawny eyes had an eager sparkle that nothing had ever been known to quench. She too smiled at Jean, a warm radiant smile, then licked her stumpy pencil and went back to the human skeleton.

Jean sat down behind the counter and looked at their unconscious backs. Then he looked at the two bow-windows of his shop, one on each side of the door, at the cobbled street outside and the moss-grown roofs of the old houses opposite outlined against the blue sky, and at the rows of sober books that lined the dim walls. A shaft of sunlight shone through a window, touched Peronelle's hair to gold and caressed the backs of the books so that colour bloomed in the shadows; blue and green and red and a sudden sparkle of gold lettering. There was no sound except Michelle's deep, absorbed breathing and the chewing sounds that Peronelle made with her pencil. The atmosphere was what the atmo-

sphere of a bookshop should be; quiet, attentive yet full
of growth; and he himself had made it what it was. . . .
Change. . . . The word was like another blow between
the eyes. Why must this beautiful thing that he had
made be swept away? Why? Why? Why? . . .
Because he was an old man and had lost the knack of
making money. . . . In his agony of mind he lifted his
clasped hands and brought them down on the counter
in front of him with a soft, despairing thud.

Both girls started and looked up, their eyes wide and
inquiring.

Jean took off his spectacles and polished them again.
He must tell them, he supposed. He would not like
them to hear of it from anyone but himself.

He told them.

When he had finished there was a horrified pause, and
their mouths fell open. . . . Jean noticed that Peronelle's pink tongue was stained black in the middle and
thought incoherently that he ought to stop her biting
her pencil in the way she did; she'd poison herself. . . .
Then Michelle on her ladder hung her head and dragged
at her loose stockings to hide her tears, but Peronelle
the practical leapt to her feet and stamped her foot in
a fury of indignation.

"Sell the shop?" she cried.

"Yes," said Jean.

"And live with that vile nephew of yours? I *hate*
your nephew! Strait-laced prig!"

"Er—yes," said Jean.

"You can't do it!" stormed Peronelle. "I tell you
you can't do it! You'd be miserable!"

Jean looked at her helplessly. It was impossible to explain to her that as life goes on the things that make one miserable seem so often to be the things that one must do.

"And we shan't be able to come and read here any more!" said Michelle in a strangled voice. "And I'm not half-way through *Agamemnon* and I've not even started the *Eumenides*!"

"Selfish beast!" stormed her sister, sending a withering glance ceilingwards. "What does it matter about your horrid *Agamemnons*? They were a loathsome set of murdering sweeps, anyway, and you wouldn't read about them if you hadn't got such a nasty mind. . . . Come down and stop snivelling. . . . What matters is poor M'sieur Garis being turned out of his bookshop," and she leapt the counter like a kangaroo and flung her arms round Jean in a hug so vehement that the shock of it sent his black skull-cap flying and exposed the place on the top of his head that had let him down. . . . And, surprisingly, so warm and consoling was her love that he did not care.

"I tell you it shan't happen," said Peronelle, picking up his skull-cap and smacking it back on his head. "*I'll* see to it all."

Jean began to laugh in spite of himself, for her remark was so typical of Peronelle. She always thought, the young monkey, that she could do everything. Her faith in her own powers was the most colossal thing he had ever met.

Peronelle, unabashed by his laughter, had fallen into the Napoleonic attitude habitual to her; legs wide apart, brows knitted and thumb thrust into her mouth for the purposes of mastication that always seemed with her to assist mental activity.

"Yes?" he queried a little slyly.

"I haven't thought yet," she flashed at him, "but I shall have by night. I shall have one of my inspirations. . . . Here, come on, 'Chelle," and seizing her sister by her thin ankles she dragged her down the ladder with more haste than decorum.

"What are you taking me away for?" inquired Michelle from an injured heap on the floor.

"I want fresh air for my inspiration," said Peronelle. "Pull your right stocking up, 'Chelle, do. You may be clever but I'd sooner die that be seen about with your legs."

Michelle picked herself up, blew her nose, dragged at her right stocking, tore a huge hole across the knee, gave it up and advanced awkwardly and a little sullenly to old Jean. . . . She felt for him terribly, but she had not got Peronelle's blessed gift of self-expression and she did not know how to say so.

"I'm sorry," she stammered.

Jean, who understood her, smiled at her and patted her bony shoulder.

"When you are a famous Blue Stocking," he said, "I shall remember that you read *Aeschylus* in my shop."

Outside in the cobbled street Peronelle stopped, looking from the bookshop to the shop on the left where Pierre Duport had made verbena scent for fifty years,

and from there to the shop on the right where Renouvette Méturier's coloured sweets, red and pink and
striped peppermint, bloomed in their bottles like
preserved rosebuds and bumble bees.

"They will go, too," said Peronelle.   "And they will
pull down the old houses and root up the cobbles and
build modern houses and streets and St. Pierre will look
like Blackpool!"

She had never been to Blackpool, but her father had,
and the things that he said about it were not com-
plimentary.

She turned fiercely on her heel and marched off down
the street with her head in the air, Michelle trailing
after, pulling at her stockings and inquiring plaintively:
"Where are we going, 'Nelle?"

"To the harbour," said Peronelle decisively.   They
were out for the afternoon with their sandwiches and
had meant to walk round to the little bay beyond the
town and eat them there, but Peronelle always found
that her inspirations came to her at the harbour; the
stir and bustle of it seemed to wind up her mind and set
it ticking like a clock.   Michelle could not understand
this.   She did not much care for her fellow creatures
and inspiration only came to her when she had gone
away somewhere quiet by herself, but Peronelle seemed
to gain it from contact with practical living.

The cobbled street reached the bottom of the hill,
twisted round behind the Town Church and brought
them out at the harbour with its two arms stretched
out to form what was almost a circle, one of them the
pier and the other the grey mass of the fort, and within

them the smooth green water, patched with floating masses of seaweed, whose serenity was disturbed by only the very worst of the winter storms.

They ran out along the pier, hopping over coils of rope, exchanging cheerful greetings with blue-jerseyed, weather-tanned fishermen, and pausing now and then to look at the few fishing boats and yachts that lay beside the pier, the lazy water slapping their sides. It was a slack time at the harbour, for the steamer from England was not due for some while yet and it was too early for the fishing boats to start out for their night's work.

At the very end of the pier the girls sat down, with their legs dangling over the edge, and considered the sea and the sky with weather-wise eyes. It had got much colder during the last hour and quite respectable-sized waves were creaming against the pier and sending up showers of spray to damp the soles of their feet. A blanket of grey cloud had swallowed up the coast of France and was slowly creeping up the sky, while the hitherto emerald Islands had turned purple. The sea, that had been blue earlier in the day, was now a curious shade of green.

"There's a gale coming," said Michelle.

"M'm," said Peronelle. "Let's have tea."

"It isn't time," objected Michelle.

"The whole point of a picnic meal," said Peronelle, "is eating it at the wrong time. And I've got ginger biscuits in my pocket if we get hungry later on. Come on. Heave up."

Michelle heaved up and Peronelle took the packet of

sandwiches out of the capacious pocket that was supposed to live at the side of her skirt but seemed somehow always to twist round to the back.

"There!" exclaimed Peronelle, "you've sat on them again!"

"Never mind," consoled Michelle. "Food gets all pulpy after it gets inside your mouth, so it might just as well do it before and save one trouble."

"Teeth decay," said Peronelle wisely, undoing the package, "unless they gnaw. Look! Mother's given us that revolting seed cake no one would eat last week! If I didn't adore Mother so much I'd say it was downright mouldy of her."

But with the sea wind in their faces and the waves breaking at their feet it did not taste so bad, and only one piece was thrown to the grey gulls who wheeled and dipped around them, mewing like kittens, their great blades of wings rising and falling rhythmically.

"They're like Aeschylus' eagles," said Michelle. "'In anguish lonely, eddying wide, great wings like oars in a waste of sky,'" and she fished a little Greek dictionary out of her pocket.

"Oh, shut up about the *Agamemnons*!" implored Peronelle. "Be quiet, do, while I memorize the position of these finger bones," and she fished a little book on anatomy out of hers, together with the nasty pile of bones which, on closer inspection, proved to be those of the human hand.

They were deep in these works when Roger Fairless, clad in the immaculate white ducks he had bought in Savile Row, strolled down the pier and stood waiting while Hélier Falliot, one of the blue-clad fishermen, got his boat ready. Hands in pockets, he surveyed them with amusement. What odd-looking little scraps they were, clothed in those unbecoming skirts and blue jerseys, with their ruffled hair in those frightful tight plaits and their long legs dangling over the pier. Shabby little paper books were held in front of their noses and their lips moved as they muttered to themselves. He strolled up beside them, but they took not the slightest notice. . . . He had never seen such absorption. . . . They'd fall in in a minute if they weren't careful.

"Aren't you two a bit near the edge?" he inquired, gazing benevolently down on them from his six feet of splendid height.

The elder girl did not even hear him. . . . Muttering, she turned a page. . . . But the younger one glanced up, looked him up and down, noted that he was English, thought little of him for that reason and hastened to put him in his place. "Fall in?" she inquired contemptuously. "We were born on this Island." Then she also turned a page and, muttering, became reabsorbed in her book.

He strolled behind them and looked over their shoulders. Great Scot! Anatomy and Greek! Really, from what he had seen of them, the natives of this Island were of a species so peculiar as to merit being put on show in the Zoological Gardens. He withdrew a little and gazed at the horizontal plaits sticking out on each side of Peronelle's golden head. . . . A beautiful little head. . . . That girl would one day be a beautiful woman. . . . He felt piqued, for he himself was no mean specimen of the human race and always attracted a good deal of notice in his native country; yet on this pier he seemed to be attracting none whatever.

"Ready, m'sieur," called Hélier from below, and held up a hand to steady him down the treacherous steps, slimy with a carpet of squelching green seaweed, into the boat. "The wind is rising, m'sieur," he cautioned. "Dirty weather coming."

"Thank you," said Roger politely, "but there's very little about sailing that I don't know. . . ." And he hoped those two indifferent girls up there had heard.

Apparently they had, for as the wind filled his sail and the little boat bounded joyously out to sea he was aware that two heads were lifted and that three pairs of eyes—Hélier Falliot was standing behind the girls—were following his progress. . . . They should see that even an Englishman could understand boats and the sea. With a satisfied smile on his face he bent to his work.

But the impression he was creating was quite other than he thought.

Hélier spat so contemptuously that no further comment upon Roger's seamanship was needed from him, and the explosiveness of his expectoration made the girls look at him reproachfully.

"Hélier!" cried Michelle, "you shouldn't have let that poor innocent out alone!"

"If he's drowned, Hélier," said Peronelle indignantly,

"it'll be your fault. Anyone could tell, by the way he stepped into the boat, that he knew nothing at all about it. He's one of those Englishmen who has done all his sailing on a place they call the Norfolk Broads. . . . I believe it's a sort of pond."

Hélier, shrugging his shoulders, opened his hands wide in a wicked gesture, and his white teeth, the gold rings in his ears and his black eyes flashed in his bronzed face. "I caution m'sieur," he said in the Island patois, "and I insist that m'sieur pay me for the boat before leaving the harbour—so——"

Again that wicked shrug and gesture of the mobile hands and Hélier Falliot, a song on his lips, strolled in the direction of the "Spouting Whale", the tavern beside the church, and the meat tea with which he kept up his strength at this hour.

"Well!" gasped Michelle, following his nonchalant form with horror-struck eyes. "Talk about a murderer."

"Your *Agamemnons*," said Peronelle, choking with indignation, "are nothing to him!"

She turned her eyes seawards again, following that dancing sail with real anxiety. She knew all about sailing—the du Frocq children could almost have been said to have been born in boats—and she knew quite well that the man out there was not equal to his job.

"'Nelle!" cried Michelle in sudden horror. "That's the man who came to see father yesterday!"

"What?" said Peronelle.

"I couldn't think at first where I'd seen him before.

81

I saw him through the kitchen window, yesterday, when you were out."

"What did he come to see father for? Who is he?" demanded Peronelle.

"He's Mr. Fairless, the new junior partner in father's firm."

"The firm that publishes father's books? Blenkinsop and Garland?" cried Peronelle, leaping to her feet.

"Yes. It's Blenkinsop, Garland and Fairless now."

There was an appalled, horrified silence. The children of literature as they were, and not without literary aspirations of their own, Michelle and Peronelle regarded publishers as the gods upon Olympus. To drown a man was bad enough but to drown a publisher was a crime for which there could be no expiation.

"It's our fault," whispered Michelle. "We shouldn't have let him go."

"A fat lot of notice he'd have taken of us if we'd told him not to," retorted Peronelle. "He's the sort that think they know everything."

They stood and watched the inexperienced yachtsman battling with the freshening wind and their pigtails quivered with horror. They glanced back over their shoulders and saw that the pier was deserted. All the fishermen had gone to their teas. In another hour, when the steamer would be due, the pier would be crowded, but now, if any unfortunate situation should arise Michelle and Peronelle du Frocq would have to cope with it single-handed.

A sudden rush of wind, the herald of the gale, flung

the seagulls skyward and tossed the crests of the green waves to foaming white. The effect was like the first spurt of wind before a thunderstorm, that passing over a green forest lifts all the leaves so that their pale undersides show in a white panic.

"He's over!" said Michelle.

He was. His puffed, conceited little white sail was suddenly not sure of itself, wavered before the wind, bowed to its majesty and was annihilated.

"Quick! Quick!" gasped Peronelle, slipping and sprawling down the slimy green steps to Hélier's small rowing boat that lay below them, and feeling in her pocket as she went for the immense jack-knife that she always carried about to sharpen her stumpy pencil with. Michelle followed after, falling her length and bursting both her in any case most inadequate garters.

They seized an oar each and glided out from the smooth harbour water into the open sea beyond. The sky, now, was all swallowed up in racing grey clouds and it was very cold. Yet in spite of the waves and the wind the little boat shot ahead at a good pace. Michelle and Peronelle might be thin but they were wiry, and they had handled oars ever since they could remember.

The Greek dictionary and the book on anatomy, left behind on the pier, flapped their pages in dismay and were finally lifted by the wind and sent whirling up to join the mewing seagulls.

Roger Fairless could swim, and indeed fancied himself as an exponent of that art, but he was so entangled in

83

ropes that he could not free himself. He could only cling to the capsized boat and hope someone had seen him. He tried to keep cool but a mounting, red-hot panic seemed slowly eating up his brain. To die held fast in a trap was to his mind the worst kind of death. . . . He always let rabbits out of traps when he had the chance. . . . There seemed a screaming sound in his head like the screaming of a trapped rabbit.

Then above the sounds of wind and water, and the noises in his own head, he heard the grating of oars in rowlocks, and looking up saw a rowing boat tossing beside him, with two small heads peering at him over the gunnel. Heavens! Those kids!

Then the little one, the fair one with the beautiful head, leaned over him brandishing a gigantic jack-knife. For a moment, so fierce was the determination in her eyes, he thought she was going to cut his throat, but she seemed to think better of it and attacked his ropes instead. . . . He was amazed at her skill. . . . She seemed to know exactly where they had entangled him and slashed away with great jabs of the knife that had him free in no time.

"Now!" she called, and four small hands grabbed him and pulled and heaved with apparently the strength of Hercules. With a flop and a squelch he rolled over the gunnel and lay prone at the bottom of the boat, like some huge moribund whale. When he recovered sufficiently to pull himself together and look up it was to see the younger girl squatting beside him and fishing various horrible-looking objects out of her capacious pocket. . . . A messy tangle of string. A stumpy, chewed pencil. The skeleton of a human hand and a couple of soggy ginger biscuits. . . . These last she disentangled from the bones and held out to him.

"Eat them," she commanded. "They'll do you good."

Then she and her sister bent to their oars again and the boat sped over the waves back to the harbour and safety.

It was when they had reached the slimy green steps, and were propelling the still bewildered Roger up them, that Michelle realized Peronelle had suddenly had one of her inspirations. . . . The signs were unmistakable. . . . Her usually pale face was rosy, her eyes were sparkling more than usual and the small, damp kiss-me-quick curls that clung all round her face and nestled at the back of her neck between her plaits looked unusually smug and self-satisfied. Michelle said nothing but waited meekly to follow where 'Nelle might lead.

Roger was marched along the pier at a smart pace, a girl on either side holding an arm each with the utmost firmness.

"I can quite well walk alone, thank you," he said, slightly nettled. . . . Really, he felt like a prisoner being marched to his cell.

"We are taking you," said Peronelle sternly, "to the house of a friend of ours in La Rue Lihou. . . . He will dry you."

"But there's no need to trouble your friend," protested Roger. "I'm staying with General Carew, you

85

know, and his dogcart is waiting for me at the 'Spouting Whale'."

"You are coming with us to La Rue Lihou," repeated Peronelle, and the gleam in her eye was ominous.

So for purposes of their own they *had* taken him prisoner. In sheer gratitude he supposed he must submit. . . . And the younger girl was really amazingly pretty. . . . Those curls in the back of her neck, now. He'd like to make further acquaintance with them.

"I'm intensely grateful," he gasped, as they rounded the Town Church at the double.

"Don't mention it," said Peronelle graciously. "My sister and I wouldn't dream of letting a publisher drown. . . . We may need you later. . . . We write."

"Oh?" gasped Roger politely. "What do you write?"

"I have just finished my autobiography," said Peronelle. "And my sister is writing a thesis on the relation of Greek tragedy to the problems of modern life."

"Oh," said Roger.

They had reached the almost perpendicular steepness of La Rue Lihou and climbed for a few moments in a panting silence.

"Have you private means?" asked Peronelle suddenly, when they stopped for a moment to get their breath.

"What?" gasped Roger.

"Have you private means? Money of your own,

apart from what you earn as a publisher, that you could spend on a rather expensive hobby?"

"Why—yes," said the bewildered Roger.

"I thought so," said Peronelle triumphantly. "I could tell by the cut of your trousers. . . . Come on."

It would be difficult to say which was more embarrassed, old Jean or Roger, when the latter was presented to Jean in the bookshop with the command that he should be instantly dried and arrayed in Jean's best. . . . However, when Peronelle said a thing was to be done, it was done, and Jean led his blushing visitor up the twisting stairs to his attic bedroom without any demur.

When Roger came downstairs again, feeling an utter fool and clad in Jean's funeral blacks, several sizes too small for him although they had been made twenty years ago in the days when old Jean was a good deal stouter than he was now, he found that the old man and the two girls had lit the fire in the sitting-room behind the shop and were preparing an Island tea. The firelight danced gaily on the brightly patterned china and the old copper pots on the dark oak dresser, while in the window the geraniums were like a second fire against the grey waste of sky and sea. The gale was on them in good earnest now but the thud of it against the window panes, and its rush and roar over the roof, seemed only to intensify the snugness of the little room. Peronelle chattered like a starling as she split open the thick, spongy, spiced Island biscuits and spread on them butter the colour of marigolds, and in a few minutes

Roger had forgotten to feel a fool and was washing lettuce in the back kitchen as though the little house had been his all his life.

The tea was such a tea as is only eaten in the Channel Islands. . . . The aforesaid spiced biscuits. Gâche, a particularly ravishing form of sultana cake. Tea, taken with cream and a very great deal of sugar. Lobster. Crab. Lettuce. Three kinds of jam. Ham. Curds. Home-made bread and a plateful of intriguing little fancy cakes called Jersey Wonders. . . . Some of it Jean had had in the house to start with and the rest Peronelle had hastily borrowed from Renouvette Méturier and Pierre Duport, that the Island be not shamed in front of an Englishman. By the time they had finished it, cleared it away and drawn their chairs round the fire, with the lamp lighted and the flowered curtains drawn between them and the storm, they were all four friends for life.

"M'sieur Jean Garis has lived here most of his life," said Peronelle to Roger, who was sitting beside her, "but now his shop does not pay any more, so he is to be turned out and all his books are to be sold."

Jean flushed painfully and his hands trembled. . . . He wished Peronelle would not expose his shame to this young man. . . . It is bitter to be shamed before the young.

"What!" cried Roger in horror, and removing from his mouth the pipe he was smoking he bent over to knock it out against the grate so that he should not look at old Jean until old Jean had had time to recover himself. . . . And he was upset himself. . . . This little house and its owner had taken his fancy in an extraordinary way. The dark, musty bookshop with its orderly rows of sober books, the bright little sitting-room with its scarlet geraniums and view of sky and sea, the copper pots and bright fire; and above all the old man himself, so courteous and dignified and kindly. . . . That these things should be parted and rent asunder was a crime of the first order.

He came painfully out of his reverie to find Peronelle stamping on his foot. . . . Not that he needed that prompting.

"What an amazing coincidence!" he said to Jean, straightening himself. Jean, now quite recovered, raised his delicate eyebrows in polite inquiry.

"I come to stay here fairly often," lied Roger glibly, "for General Carew is my cousin; and I've got a great wish to own a bookshop in the Channel Islands. . . . I'm a publisher, as you know. . . . The difficulty is to find the shop and a manager who will look after it for me in my absence. I do not want a commercially minded man, you understand, for this shop will be a hobby, not a means of livelihood, I want a man who loves books as I do."

There was a silence, while old Jean gripped the arms of his chair with his blue-veined hands and his eyes never left the young man's face.

Roger leaned towards him, gently, pleadingly, hesitating and diffident, his attitude the reverential one of a disciple before his master.

"Heavens! What an actor!" thought the jubilant Peronelle.

"Could you consider helping me out, sir," he asked humbly. "Is there any chance that you yourself would—er——"

The rain had begun now and was pattering sharply against the window panes behind the flowered curtains, while over the roof the wind roared like a monster; but to old Jean Garis there was no longer any terror in the storm.

Chapter Four

THE NEW MOON

What had she done, thought Rachell du Frocq, to be cursed with these appalling children? She doubted if there was any mother on the Island, or indeed upon any of these islands that lay like jewels in the English Channel, or in England or France either for that matter, who had such quarrelsome children as hers; particularly in the weeks after Christmas. They had been good children before Christmas and angels throughout its exhausting festivities, but now, just when their father had fallen ill and she had her hands more than full, they must turn overnight into complete and utter demons. She looked at them with disfavour as they sat in a row in front of her at the shoemaker's, having new school boots tried on, and wondered from whom they had inherited their vile tempers; not from their father, poor lamb, whose sweetness of disposition not even bronchitis complicated by an overdrawn bank balance had been able seriously to disturb; and not from her, for goodness knew she had the patience of a saint under trials and afflictions that would have ground a lesser woman to pulp; she didn't know who they got them from.

"For goodness' sake, Michelle!" she stormed at her

eldest, her magnificent dark eyes flashing and her shapely foot tapping the floor impatiently. "Make up your mind one way or the other. You must know which boots pinch and which don't."

"They *all* pinch," said Michelle, glowering over her spectacles at her mother. "I wish I could wear sandals, like the ancient Greeks. I wish I *was* an ancient Greek."

"Well, you aren't," snapped Rachell. "You are a disagreeable little Channel Island girl of the nine-teenth century. And I can't sit here all the afternoon. Hurry up, dear, do. Here are all the rest of you horrid little creatures to be shod before we can get home and have a little peace."

"Now, don't get in one of your rages, Mother," admonished Peronelle, "you'll only make her worse. Keep calm, darling, and think how dreadful it would be if you had ten children to shoe instead of only five."

Rachell began to laugh in spite of herself, and eyed them with less disfavour than formerly; Michelle, plain, bespectacled, and clever; Peronelle, vivid and im-pulsive, with golden curls framing a heart-shaped face; Jacqueline, dark and pretty and inclined to pessimism; Colin, the only boy, lithe and brown and compact of wickedness; Colette, the baby, round and fat and fair and adorable. . . . Yet to-day even Colette's lower lip stuck out, and her forehead scowled. . . . The ex-hausted shop assistant put the tenth pair of boots on to Michelle's extended feet, and the quarrel went on again from where it had momentarily left off.

"I tell you there *are* fairies!" shouted Colette.

"There aren't," mocked Colin, "and only silly little babies like you think there are."

"I'm *not* a silly baby," said Colette, and stuck out her lower lip even further.

"If you don't hold your tongue, Colin," said Peronelle, "it'll be the worse for you in another couple of minutes," and she tossed back her curls as a warhorse his mane.

"There are fairies, Mother, aren't there?" pleaded Colette. "You've always said there were."

"Perhaps, darling," said Rachell absently. "Now do be quiet and let poor Mademoiselle get on with the fitting. Your turn, Jacqueline."

"I wish I was dead," said Jacqueline suddenly. The sight of her new school boots reminded her of the return to school next week, and her heart seemed to fall into her stomach.

"Selfish pig," said Peronelle. "Think of the expense your funeral would be to Father."

Colette looked at Jacqueline with large hazel eyes full of reproach. "And Father and Mother love you," she lisped sweetly. "People like to have little girls."

"Conceited little beast," said Colin scornfully. "So you think silly little girls who believe in fairies are nice, do you? Well, they aren't. They're the scum of the earth. I have four sisters, and I should know."

Colette wept.

Peronelle, whose special pet her little sister was, leaped to her feet in flaming indignation and flung herself upon her brother. They rolled over on the floor, biting and scratching. Colette, still roaring, flew to

Peronelle's assistance, and Jacqueline joined in just for company. Boots flew in the air like hailstones, and the terrified shop assistant leaped for safety like a kangaroo. . . . Only Michelle remained aloof in spectacled superiority. "Something is rotten in the state of Denmark," she observed sententiously.

Rachell arose in her wrath, her worn black dress and cloak swirling around her like the robes of a Cleopatra, and her head held as proudly as though the shabby bonnet that sat on her coiled dark hair were a golden crown. "Stop that instantly," she said, and bending over the combatants dragged them apart with a vigour and skill born of long and arduous practice.

"What a woman!" thought the admiring assistant, picking up boots. "She's like a duchess. She oughtn't to have to wear those shabby clothes and look after those awful children herself."

Rachell, as she shook and dusted her offspring, was thinking exactly the same thing with the part of her mind that lay below the surface and to whose remarks she was generally careful not to listen. She was remembering the days of her youth, the days when she had been the beauty of the Island and had become engaged to Sebastian de la Rue, a man some years older than herself but possessed of dazzling good looks, a pride and temper to match her own, and a fortune that had taken away the breath of her ambitious parents. She had jilted him; thrown away all the great possessions that might have been hers to marry André du Frocq, a penniless poet-farmer whose gentleness and charm had for once in her life bound her pride with

chains. She regretted her marriage only on the rare
occasions when her strength failed a little under the
burden of a delicate husband, noisy children, and that
hampering poverty that made her unable to do for
them all that she would. Funny, she thought, as she
straightened her scowling offspring and placed them
again on their chairs, that after all these years she
should think again of Sebastian. He had come back
to the Island, she had heard, after a successful career in
diplomacy, and bought a fine house in this town of
Saint Pierre. Had she married him she too would have
been living now in a comfortable town house, instead
of in that cold farm on a bleak cliff-top, and the
governess would have taken the children to try their
boots on. . . . Ah, but they would not have been
André's children, and in none of them would there have
been that charm and sweetness (not very apparent just
at the moment) that ran like a golden streak through the
characters of all of them, and had come to full flower in
baby Colette.

The reverie was abruptly interrupted by the dis-
covery that Colette had disappeared.

Colette was a good and a patient child, but there are
times when even a worm will turn. Colin's unpleasant
remarks about the nastiness of little girls had of course
cut her to the heart, but it was not so much the remarks
that had sent her rushing out into the street as the sudden
hacking away of the roots of her belief. . . . Her faith
in fairies had been until this moment the foundation
stone of her existence. . . . She had been one of the true

believers, one of those to whom their faith is of such value that beside it all other possessions become a mere encumbrance, and now that it had been taken from her she was a lost soul. It had not been Colin who had destroyed her faith, it had been Rachell with her careless "Perhaps. . . ." Colette was old enough to know that one did not answer in that sort of way about what was really true.

Her instinct for flight had carried her right down the street before she knew where she was. The cold winter dusk was drawing in, and the pavements were almost deserted, for most people had gone home to tea. She turned a corner and ran down another street, her small booted feet making a trotting sound on the hard frosted pavement, like those of a sturdy pony, and her plump little figure in its bunchy dark blue overcoat looking as broad as it was long. Fair kiss-me-quick curls framed her face under her scarlet tam-o'-shanter, and larger curls, of the sausage variety, lay in the nape of her neck. Her nose was slightly *retroussé*, and her face was as round and pink as an opened wild rose. She had neither the face nor the figure for tragedy, and no one, to look at her, could have guessed what she was feeling. . . . Indeed there were very few people who did not smile as she passed them. . . . The passage of Colette through the world was like that; she left smiles behind her, and a lightening of the heart.

Colette's legs, though plump, had always been inadequate to her weight, and presently they ached a good deal and she had a stitch in her side. She had turned two more corners, and she did not know where she was.

She stopped, for she was suddenly very bewildered. "Please, God, find me," she demanded, and her eyes went anxiously up and down the street, as though she expected to see her guardian angel rushing along to the rescue.

But she saw instead a smart brougham drawn up at the side of the kerb, outside a tobacconist's shop, with a statuesque coachman, whose face she could not see behind his turned-up collar, sitting on the box staring absent-mindedly into vacancy. It was Grandfather's brougham with its door wide open, gaping for her! With a squeal of delight she scampered to it, scrambled in, and cuddled up in a dark corner, giggling deliciously. Presently her Grandfather, the doctor, would come out of the tobacconist's and get in, and then she would bounce out, and he would roar with laughter into his big beard.

But it was not Grandfather who came out of the tobacconist's, it was an entirely strange footman carrying a couple of long boxes of cigars. He flung them carelessly on to the seat beside Colette, jumped up beside the coachman, and they were off, the brougham swaying and rattling over the cobbles that paved the narrow street.

Colette stopped giggling and began to suck her thumb in some consternation. . . . It wasn't Grandfather's brougham after all. . . . She wasn't frightened, for she was a courageous little girl, but she did wonder where on earth she was going to. She came out of her corner and sat in the centre of the seat; it was so wide that her fat legs stuck out horizontally in front of her, and she found something reassuring in the sight of her muddy boots and scratched bare knees. She always had the feeling that her legs were not part of her but were two friendly little elves who did her bidding and carried her about. Now she waggled them from side to side and dimpled at them, and they seemed to laugh back at her. If the worst came to the worst, they said, they would help her to run away.

She felt better now and began to notice the strange magic world through which she was passing. . . . For night had come, the lamplighter had passed like a glow-worm up hill and down dale, and its hour of enchantment was upon this town of Saint Pierre. . . . The black jumble of roofs and chimneys, falling so steeply down the rocky cliff to the sea, were only visible as queer crazy shapes like witches' hands reaching up to pluck the stars out of the sky, and below them the narrow twisting streets were deep clefts in the rock where hobgoblins lurked. The lighted windows of the houses were squares and oblongs of orange and amber and deep scarlet, flowers embroidered on the train of night, while here and there the starlight shone on a sparkle of frost upon a roof or a swirl of mysteriously illumined smoke. . . . Surely in such a world as this there are fairies. Surely news of an invisible world is written plain for all to see in the charactery of lights upon the darkness and stars in the sky.

Like the coach that carried Cinderella to the ball the brougham rolled on and on, into the pools of light that lay around the lamps and out again into the darkness that was lapping up between the walls of the houses

like the waves of the sea. It seemed hours before it
stopped with a jolt beside a door in a wall, with steps
leading up to it and a great iron bell hanging down
beside it. When the footman jumped down and
pulled it, it pealed out menacingly, as Colette had known
it would, and she leaned forward anxiously, expecting
to see at least a gnome or an ogre come out of the door.
... For the moment she had forgotten that there were
no such things.

But nothing worse came out than a large bald butler.

"Dropped them luncheon visitors in the town,
George?" he inquired. "Got them cigars?"

The footman grunted an affirmative and flung open
the door of the brougham, disclosing Colette. His jaw
dropped, and his eyes bulged so that he looked more
like a frog than anything except a frog that Colette had
ever seen. "'Ere, Mr. 'Iggins," he gasped. "You
come 'ere and 'ave a look at this."

Mr. Higgins came and looked, and so did the coachman. They all three stared with their mouths open,
like fishermen who have hooked a mermaid up out of
the sea.

"I didn't never see 'er get in, Frank, did you?" said
George to the coachman, and the coachman, removing
his top hat and scratching his head perplexedly, said no,
he was blessed if he had.

"Ask 'er where she come from and take 'er back,"
suggested Mr. Higgins.

But Colette had no intention of being taken back to
where she had come from, for through the open door she
had seen inside that house and it was the loveliest house

imaginable. At sight of it the spirit of adventure was born in her, and she forgot everything but her desire to get inside. . . . There were great pots of flowers in there; chrysanthemums and tall arum lilies and cyclamens like pink and white butterflies. . . . She wriggled forward so that she could get her legs down, climbed out of the brougham, walked across the pavement and up the steps into the house. It was a full three minutes before Mr. Higgins could pull himself together sufficiently to hurry after her.

He found her standing beside an arum lily, stroking its long velvet tongue with a gentle forefinger.

"And 'oo might you be?" he demanded.

"Colette Henriette Marie-Louise du Frocq," said that lady, and gave him her loveliest smile.

Mr. Higgins was knocked all of a heap. He, together with the footman and coachman, had only recently been imported from England and he could not get used either to the unexpected behaviour of the Islanders or to their outlandish names. Like one in a dream he flung open a door and announced her.

"Mademoiselle Colette Henriette Marie-Louise du Frocq."

Colette walked in.

"And to what am I indebted for the honour of this visit?" asked the tall man who stood on the white bearskin rug in front of the fire.

"I just came," said Colette. "Please may I take my coat off?"

Being the baby of the family, with three adoring elder sisters, Colette was not used to disrobing herself

"'ERE, MR. 'IGGINS," HE GASPED, "YOU COME 'ERE
AND 'AVE A LOOK AT THIS."

without assistance. She stood holding her arms out
wide and looking appealingly up at her host until he
realized what was expected of him and came to the
rescue. . . . She was so fat, and her coat so much too
tight for her, that it was like skinning a rabbit.

"Now my boots," said Colette cheerfully, and sitting down on a chair beside the fire she extended her
feet toward him. He was not used to children, and he
fumbled clumsily with the intricacy of knots and laces,
but Colette was an angel of patience. "You'll do it
better next time," she said.

When at last he had got them off he sat down on the
chair opposite and looked at her. She wore a diminu-
tive frock the colour of a holly berry, with a white frill
round the neck that set off her glowing face like the
calyx of a flower. Her toes, stretched out toward the
warmth of the fire, wriggled ecstatically in joy at their
freedom. She was like a flame burning in his room, a
flame of delight.

And Colette in her turn looked at him with all her
eyes, for he was to her a new specimen of the human
race and as such worthy of her interested attention. . . .
She liked people; and she preferred men to women
because she found them more obedient. . . . This one
was tall and thin and upright, as though he had swallowed a poker and his figure had become moulded to it.
There was something rather rigid about his face too,
with its hard lines running from nose to mouth, but on
the whole he was nice to look at, with crinkles in his
grey hair, beautiful clothes, and a peculiarly attractive
eyeglass in one eye, attached to his person by a glossy

ribbon. Colette decided that she liked him, and smiled.

"Do we have tea now?" she suggested.

The man leaned forward and pulled the bell.

"Muffins," said Colette, "and honey."

"I am yours to command," said her host. Colette beamed again. She liked this man more and more.

"Tea, Higgins," he said, when that worthy appeared. "And muffins and honey."

"We 'aven't got no 'oney in the 'ouse, sir," said Higgins, slightly aggrieved.

"Then send out for it," snapped his master. "Send George."

"Very good, sir," and Higgins withdrew.

There was now an interval, while George fetched the honey, employed by Colette in an account of the history and habits of the du Frocq family. She had not yet discovered that the farmhouse of Bon Repos was not the hub of the universe, round which all interest centred. . . . And indeed people usually were very interested in Colette's account of what the du Frocq's had had for breakfast, for it is the personality of the teller rather than the actual news retailed that gives spice to conversation. . . . And this man was more than interested. He was thrilled. The very mention of the word du Frocq seemed to give him an electric shock. He sat forward in his chair, his clasped hands dropped between his knees and his eyes fixed upon Colette as though she had brought him news from a far country. "Yes?" he kept saying. "Yes? And is your mother well? Five children did you say? And your father ill? Good heavens! . . . And do they think you're like your mother?"

"No," said Colette. "I'm fair like Father, but I get my fat from Aunt Sophia Antoinette Marguerite du Putron. . . . She had five chins."

"Nevertheless," murmured the man to himself. "She is like. . . . The imperiousness; the habit of command."

At this moment the commanded muffins and honey appeared, accompanied by pale amber tea in a beautiful teapot of Worcester china, cream and milk in silver jugs, and sugar cakes upon a lordly dish; and Colette spoke no more.

She was in the middle of her sixth muffin when she suddenly burst into floods of tears. The luxuries she had been enjoying, the lilies and the cyclamens, the muffins and silver jugs and honey-pots, had for a while made her forget the tragedy of the afternoon, but now she remembered it and knew these things for what they were, only the vanities of this world that were but dust and ashes beside the lost treasure of her faith. . . . There were no fairies. . . . She howled and howled.

Monsieur de la Rue was deeply distressed. A difficult international situation he could deal with, but a weeping child was outside his province altogether. But he did his best. He lifted Colette clumsily upon his knees and implored her to be comforted. . . . She was comforted. . . . She leaned her head against his shoulder, and her sobs died away into pathetic hiccups. "Blow my nose," she whispered. Horribly embarrassed, Monsieur de la Rue took his beautiful white silk handkerchief from his pocket and advanced it gingerly toward that *retroussé* member. Colette, however, did her part. She buried her face in his handkerchief, made a noise like a foghorn, and the thing appeared to be done. Sighing with relief he put his handkerchief away again and endeavoured to put her down.

Colette, however, did not wish to be put down; she wanted to stay where she was and explain exactly why it was she was so unhappy. The only enjoyment to be got out of affliction, she had long ago discovered, was the telling people about it over and over again, making it worse every time; and lapping up their sympathy as a kitten cream.

And Sebastian de la Rue, the wealthy bachelor diplomatist, a man reputed to be as unimaginative as he was brilliant and as callous as he was subtle, understood Colette as few other people would have done. For he had once lived in a fairy tale. He had once possessed a treasure of such price that the loss of it had turned all subsequent possession to bitterness. He remembered as though it were yesterday a dinner at the Governor's, and Rachell standing before him on the terrace in the moonlight, drawn to her full height, facing a difficult situation with her usual rather cruel directness and grit. "I am sorry," she had said, "but I can't. I never really loved you. You are too proud and too passionate. We are too alike to be happy together." And she had gone away and left him, walking slowly down the terrace with her head held high and the folds of her elaborate white satin evening dress swirling magnificently round her. . . . And he had stood there, looking stupidly at the emerald she had left lying on the palm of his hand, overwhelmed by mental pain so fierce that it had crept through every fibre of his body as though he had been stretched upon the rack. . . . In after years he had come to think that she was right, that a union of two such imperious tempers would have led to tragedy, but that made no difference to the fact that in the full flood of his happiness he had had a shock that had poisoned it for life.

And now the cycle of existence had brought her child to sit on his knee and tell him, through tears, of a fairy-tale broken.

"Personally," he said, in the cold professional tone that he used at diplomatic meetings of international importance, "I believe in fairies. The evidence to hand in favour of their existence needs sifting and tabulating, but to my mind it should be convincing to every man of moderate intelligence." Foreign diplomatists had never been able to tell whether Sebastian de la Rue was lying or not, he had deceived them at will, so it was an easy task for him to bring conviction to one small girl.

"You really, really think there are fairies?" she asked, her eyes fixed on him with her mother's direct-ness.

"I do not hesitate to give it as my profound and un-alterable conviction," said Sebastian de la Rue, "that there are fairies. . . . And you can, if you wish, prove the truth of my statement."

Colette's eyes sparkled like stars.

"We are approaching the next new moon," he continued in level tones. "I think I am right in stating that it rises to-morrow." He drew a diary from his pocket, adjusted his eyeglass, consulted it and verified his statement. "Yes. . . . When the moon shines through your window you should salute her as doubtless in common with all other Island children you have been taught to do, and then punctually upon the last stroke of nine you should concentrate your gaze upon the doorstep."

"The fairies will be there?" breathed Colette.

"They may be, or they may not," said Sebastian. "But the gifts of the moon fairies will most certainly be there. The moon never fails to reward courteous little girls who do her reverence and believe in fairies."

Colette dropped her head against his shoulder with a sigh of happiness. "I think," she said, "that I could finish that muffin now."

She finished it and they sat together in the firelight in complete accord for a long time. Then, as a log fell and a shower of bright sparks went up the chimney like a company of stars, Sebastian roused himself and rang the bell.

"You must permit me," he said to Colette, "to send you home in my carriage."

Rachell could make neither head nor tail of Colette's account of the afternoon's adventures. Out of a jumble of arum lilies, muffins, eyeglasses, and someone called 'Iggins nothing very definite emerged except the fact that Rachell herself, by a careless chance remark, had destroyed Colette's belief in fairies, and that an entirely unknown man (not, apparently, 'Iggins), had restored it again by concocting for her a pretty tale of moon fairies and gifts upon the doorstep. Rachell, sitting in front of the kitchen fire and nursing a Colette warm and rosy from her bath, was overwhelmed by penitence for her own misdemeanour and gratitude to the unknown. She had spent a frightful afternoon— they had all spent a frightful afternoon—hunting for Colette, but now, with her precious babe restored to her, and André, to-night, quite definitely round the corner, anxiety and bad temper were things of the past and she was once again the gracious, adoring, indulgent mother whom her children knew best. Colette nestled close, aware that with Mother in this mood, and with a little guile on her part, bedtime could be postponed quite indefinitely.

"What will the moon fairies give me, Mother?" she asked. "Will it be something to eat?"

"Greedy little pig!" laughed Rachell.

"I'm not!" said Colette indignantly. "I should give it all to Father to make him fat."

"Darling little lamb!" said Rachell, and kissed Colette in the back of her neck, under her sausage curls.

Then anxiety overwhelmed her. If Colette, to-morrow night, were to open the front door as the clock was striking nine and find nothing on the doorstep then her faith would be shattered for the second time; and this time for good. It was a difficult problem, this business of guiding the feet of little children as they pattered out of the path of "let's pretend" into the stony road of hard fact. She thought it would break her heart if any child of hers should ever echo Cleopatra's bitter words: "There is nothing left remarkable beneath the visiting moon." For as long as possible the moon must stand to Colette for romance and the radiance of fairy gifts. But would this unknown man see that it did? Would he rise to the occasion that he had himself created?

"You know, darling," she said anxiously to Colette, "if you open the door to-morrow night and find nothing on the doorstep you must not think that means that there are no fairies. The fairies, poor little dears, are very overworked at the time of the new moon, and they can't be everywhere at once."

"Oh yes they can," said Colette, nodding wisely at the fire. "And to-morrow night there will be lots of things to eat upon the doorstep. . . . There might," she added wistfully, "be enough for me as well as Father."

The night of nights arrived, and Rachell was in an agony. She had half a mind to put some eatables out on the doorstep herself, but there was nothing in the larder that could be spared except the mutton bone and a few stewed prunes, and Colette hated prunes. As the fatal hour drew on her presence was demanded by André, who had now arrived at that stage of convalescence when returning energy takes the form of keeping one's nurse upon the run in a perpetual, but hopeless, search for the right book to suit the mood of the moment. As she ransacked shelves and cupboards, replying patiently, "Yes, darling," to André's querulous "I can't remember the name but you must know the one I mean," her ears were strained to catch the slightest sound in the quiet night that was folding Bon Repos in its peace. . . . At about a quarter to nine she thought she heard a trotting horse, but she could not be certain. . . . And then André upset his supper tray all over the bed, and Colette was momentarily forgotten.

She stood in the middle of the kitchen floor, still dressed in her holly-red dress, for Rachell had said she might stay up as long as she liked. The fire had died down, and there was no light in the kitchen but that of the blazing stars and the new moon. It was one of those great nights of utter stillness when beneath the glory of the sky the earth seems to shrink to a mere nothing, a tiny pensioner crouching at the feet of night. . . . The friendly earth that was to Colette just this little Island, with its rocky cliffs and green lanes a setting for the old farmhouse where she lived in such content, with the sea all round her as a friend by day and night. . . . She could hear it now, a murmuring voice in the darkness. She was not afraid of the sea, not even during nights of storm, for Bon Repos was so near it that its voice was the first thing she had heard when she came into the world.

And now the new moon claimed her attention. It seemed to hang just outside the kitchen window, a thin crescent of perfection whose radiance, added to that of the stars, played with the shadows in the corners of the room and called out answering lights in the warming pans and old copper pots that were ranged round the white-washed walls.

Colette did as all the Island children were taught to

do from their babyhood up. She held up her red skirt on either side and curtsied three times to the moon. "*Je vous salue, belle lune*," she said. "*Je vous salue.*"

She was still squatting on the stone-flagged floor, with the faint moonlight pouring over her, when the old grandfather clock began to strike. She stayed where she was, crouched in homage, and counted the strokes on her fat fingers.

"Nine!"

She jumped up and ran like the wind out of the kitchen and down the passage to the front door. When the doorstep was revealed she was so excited that she could hardly see and had to rub her fists in her eyes to clear her sight. . . . Then she saw.

Her shrieks and squeals of joy brought the whole family running pell-mell. André, suddenly deserted by Rachell without a word of apology, sat up in bed and wondered if they had all gone mad, for even for his noisy family the hubbub going on downstairs passed all bounds.

"Grapes!" yelled Michelle. "Both sorts!"

"A bottle of wine!" triumphed Rachell. "Your father may call himself a teetotaller but he loves a little drop of something when it's a duty."

"A jelly!" shouted Peronelle. "A pink one with cherries in it."

"There's a huge bunch of flowers," cried Jacqueline. "That must be for Mother."

"A chicken!" roared Colin. "A chicken in a silver dish, with a sort of white blanket over the top and new moons on it cut out of tomato."

"Come upstairs and show it all to Father," shouted Peronelle.

"A big, big box of chocolates," squeaked Colette, staggering to her feet with the blue-ribboned trophy clasped to her breast. "I don't think, Mother, do you, that chocolates would be very good for Father?"

It was a good hour before the tumult died down and Rachell could clear the children off André's bed and pack them off to their own. It would, she thought, be kill or cure with André, but judging by his alertness of expression and the large quantity of grapes he had already disposed of she fancied it would be cure.

"Lie down, darling, for goodness' sake," she implored him, "while I go and put these flowers in water."

Down by herself in the kitchen she filled a vase for the flowers by the light of the moon. They were flowers such as she loved and had not possessed for years, great white chrysanthemums like balls of snow. She held them between her hands and sniffed their pungent scent with great breaths of delight. Then she untied the ribbon that bound them and found that one end of it was fastened securely to a little box hidden in the middle of the flowers. She opened it and took out an emerald ring.

A stone of elfin green that shone as she held it up to the moonlight. . . . She wondered where she had seen it before. . . . Then she suddenly remembered that scene on the terrace and the tall arrogant girl dressed in white satin. That had been an ignorant girl who did not know what it was to suffer, and the woman of knowledge she had become, looking back at her, hated her for her intolerable cruelty. "And yet I was right," she sighed. "But I need not have done it like that. What a pig you were, Rachell!"

She put the ring on her finger, put her flowers in water and went upstairs to bed.

The next day she went to see Sebastian. André, well through his second bunch of grapes and more than convalescent after a glass of port with his lunch, was not in the least jealous. He was as sure of his wife's love as he was sure that the moon would rise again to-night, and he considered a little sentimentality wholesome for all.

Rachell arrived at Sebastian's front door at about the same hour as Colette had done, when the lighted windows of Saint Pierre were like flowers in the night and the roofs and chimneys were dark shapes that blotted out the stars. She rang the bell with determination and was admitted by Higgins. She swept past him into the hall, her shabby black skirts swirling, and stood for a moment as Colette had done, stroking the velvet tongue of an arum lily, while Higgins cleared his throat, shot out his cuffs, opened the library door, and announced her.

"Madame du Frocq."

Sebastian, adjusting his eyeglass, rose to meet her. He had expected this visit, he had indeed fished for it with his gift of the emerald ring, but now that it was actually upon him he found that he was positively nervous. . . . Shrinking, fool that he was, from a fresh hurt.

Yet, as Rachell put her hand in his, he realized that there was no danger of it, for this middle-aged woman who stood before him was not the Rachell he had known. She was Madame du Frocq, so entirely different a person that she seemed to him a stranger. . . . He realized overwhelmingly how human beings change each other. . . . André du Frocq, with his humility that had softened her pride and his dependence upon her that had called out her tenderness, had made of Rachell a woman she would not have been had Sebastian been her husband. Sebastian had now no part in her, and the gulf between them was so wide that they had no further power to hurt each other.

But they had the right to demand of each other a sweet regretful sentiment, enjoyable as the scent of violets in a quiet garden.

"You are as beautiful as ever, dearest Rachell," lied Sebastian tenderly, pressing her hand in its worn black glove.

"Dear Sebastian," murmured Rachell, noting the hardness of his face and mentally thanking God for André, "how good it is to see you again." She paused, lowering her eyes. "I detest," she said, "the cruelty of the girl I once was."

"That," said Sebastian, "is a thing of the past."

The apology over, Rachell sighed with relief, sat down, took off her gloves, and raised her veil. "I hope," she said, "that I have struck the tea hour. I always try to."

Sebastian rang the bell. "Muffins and honey?" he asked with twinkling eyes.

Rachell looked up hastily and a little anxiously. "I do hope," she said, "that Colette was not very greedy the day before yesterday? Yes, Sebastian dear, I adore muffins."

Sebastian stood smiling down upon her, feeling extraordinarily light-hearted. "I may come to Bon Repos and be friends with you all?" he asked.

"But of course," cried Rachell. "It's a funny place, you know. It's very old, and full of children, but the front door is always wide open."

"It sounds like Fairyland," said Sebastian.

Chapter Five

PICNIC WITH ALBERT

COLIN DU FROCQ was paying a visit to Grandpapa and there was nothing he loathed more. It was true that he was accompanied by the girls, but he never had much use for the girls; or thought that he hadn't. To have no brothers was bad enough, he was apt to say, but to have four sisters was worse. . . . Not but what the girls had their uses, especially when he wanted his nails cut.

Why, he demanded of fate, had Father and Mother got to go for a holiday to England? What did they want a holiday at all for? They never did anything to tire them, as far as he could see, and they had five delightful children to keep them amused all day long, not to mention a farm with the proper complement of pigs, cows, chickens and four ducks. The worst of living on a rocky Island in the middle of the English Channel was that the parents could not leave it without being separated from their offspring by miles of stormy sea. . . . It gave a small boy a queer feeling in the pit of the stomach to think that his mother was all that way away.

He sat up in bed rather forlornly and gazed at the grey square of window. Soon, he thought, it would be daylight and then he would feel better. It was a rather chilly spring, and he didn't like the early hours of the morning in chilly weather, for he was one of those energetic sleepers who always kick their bedclothes off during the night, which though good exercise at the time is unpleasant later. . . . He was beastly cold and the room was so big and so gloomy, so different from his dear little room at home. . . . For Grandpapa, the chief doctor of the Island, lived in a large house in the town of St. Pierre, a heavy, wealthy, autocratic, dignified house that was an excellent reflection of Grandpapa himself.

Suddenly Colin wanted his mother so much that he couldn't bear it any more. He leapt from his bed and scuttled across the floor on his bare feet, padded down the passage and burst into the large, depressing bedchamber where slept his two eldest sisters, Michelle and Peronelle, in a four-poster hung with maroon velvet curtains. He took a run and a jump and landed on top of them, then wriggled his cold little body down under the blankets between their warm ones, gaining himself elbow room with vigorous sharp shoves to right and left.

They screamed and awoke.

"It's that young toad Colin," said Michelle.

"Get out, you little beast!" exclaimed Peronelle.

"I want Mother," said Colin.

Instantly the tone of his reception changed. He was given all the room he wanted and his cold toes were rubbed. He was cooed over and even kissed, though only once, because he had a habit of wiping off kisses with the back of his hand that was rather discouraging to the expression of affection. Finally, when it was time to get up, Peronelle came with him to his room to do up his braces and see that he washed behind his ears.

"What would you like to do to-day, darling?" she inquired, for it was the holidays and there was no school, a fact which made the boredom of a visit to Grandpapa more acute than ever.

"I should like," said Colin, "to go for a picnic this afternoon on L'Ancre Common with Albert the Good."

Albert was the donkey who pulled Grandpapa's mowing machine and Grandpapa, for some unknown reason, was devotedly attached to him and most reluctant to lend him to the grandchildren lest he should be overtired; which was only too likely, Albert not being as young as he had been and the grandchildren not as old as they one day would be.

"Well, perhaps," said Peronelle doubtfully. "We'll ask Grandpapa at breakfast," and gathering up the folds of her flannel dressing-gown, and shaking back her long golden ringlets, she went off to a third gloomy bedroom to see how Jacqueline and Colette were getting on. Jacqueline, though older than Colin, still had to be hooked up down the back and Colette, the baby, had been so spoilt that she needed to have nearly everything done for her. Peronelle, the beauty of the family, was also the only practical one and as such had a hard life, for Michelle was intellectual, Jacqueline was temperamental, Colin was naughty and Colette was both fat and pious, so that none of them could do anything for themselves without disastrous results.

. . . . .

118

Picnic With Albert

Breakfast was a strained and rather silent meal for Grandpapa's temper, never good at any time and always entirely dependent upon his digestion, was quite shocking after the enforced starvation of the night. Peronelle diplomatically waited until he had absorbed two eggs, four slices of toast, two cups of coffee and the leading article before she ventured to broach the subject of Albert; but even then it was not well received.

"Eh?" said Grandpapa. "What? What? Take Albert for a picnic? Certainly not."

"But Colin is missing Mother," said Peronelle, "and he'd love a picnic with Albert."

"He can picnic if he likes to," said Grandpapa. "You can all picnic and a d—er—good riddance." He stopped for a moment to clear his throat. He always tried very hard not to swear in front of the children, but it was a great strain on him. "But not with Albert. I'll not have that unfortunate animal dragged round the Island like a poodle on a string. I've said so before and I say it again. Why you children can never take no for an answer I don't know. What? What? Just like your mother. Argue, argue, argue about this, that and the other till a man's head goes round."

Grandpapa thumped his newspaper down on the table, wiped his beautiful grey beard and moustache carefully on his silk handkerchief and regarded his four elder grandchildren with early-morning disfavour. . . . A poor lot, he considered, and distressingly like his daughter-in-law. . . . Michelle was both plain and clever, and if there was one thing Grandpapa disliked more than a plain woman it was a clever one; Peronelle, though pretty, was a manager; Jacqueline, though also pretty, was nervous; and Colin was a cheeky young rascal. Only Colette was always dear to him, even in the early mornings, fat Colette with her short fair curls and sky-blue frock, her piety and her devotion to her food. He looked at her affectionately where she sat upon his left hand, eating her sixth slice of bread and honey, her cheeks flushed with health and her eyes still shining with the light of another world that had dawned there while she said her prayers before breakfast. Indulgently he poked one of his fingers through a curl, noting how the morning sun touched it to gold, while Colette, her mouth being used for purposes of mastication, smiled at him with her eyes and reached for the honey.

"Colette would love to have Albert, wouldn't you, darling?" said Peronelle, and gently kicked her small sister under the table.

Colette had been brought up never to speak with her mouth full, so it was a moment or two before she was able to wipe it and give tongue. "Not if Grandpapa would rather not," she cooed.

The others sighed in exasperation. . . . The little wretch was always letting them down like that. . . . She did not mean to, of course, for she was a darling little saint, but like many of the saints she lived so much in the other world that she seldom listened to what people were saying in this one, and also she always spoke the truth, a combination of habits that was bound to lead, sooner or later, to disaster. . . . Uncertain that anything was wrong she beamed upon them all and pursued a straying drop of honey with a long pink tongue.

"Always Grandpapa's good girl," said the infatuated old man, and inserted another lump of sugar in her milk.

"There's Dr. Atkinson starting out," said Michelle acidly, with intent to annoy Grandpapa.

"What? What?" he ejaculated, and hurried from his seat to the window, adjusting his eyeglass and growling savagely into his beard.

Dr. Atkinson was a smart young up-to-date English doctor who had dared to take a house opposite Grandpapa's and set up in a practice that bid fair to rival Grandpapa's own. For thirty years Grandpapa had held undisputed sway over all the livers on the Island and it was not to be expected that he should take this insult lying down. . . . Nor did he. . . . The things that he said about Dr. Atkinson all over the Island were unrepeatable, though naturally widely repeated. It was a fight to the death between modernity and the *status quo* and which would win the Island, watching with deep interest and betting heavily on the odds, did not yet know. . . . It would depend, of course, which doctor General Carew would call in next time he had the apoplexy.

(It should be stated here, in parenthesis, that the Carews were the aristocracy of the Island, and General Carew the head of the gang. They were the leaders in society, the supporters of charity concerts and sales of work, and the arbiters of fashion. . . . If you were cut in the street by a Carew you were done for. . . . No more need be said.)

"How early he starts out," said Peronelle wickedly.
"He must have a very large practice."

"One of you children ring the bell," choked Grandpapa. "Why are the horses not round? What?
What? I should have started on my rounds half an
hour ago but for this incessant damnable argue, argue,
argue!"

He strode from the room, swearing under his breath,
just as Dr. Atkinson in his smart dark-blue brougham
drove off down the hill. Ten minutes later the children,
crowding together at the window, cheered loudly as the
smart dark-green du Frocq brougham dashed up to the
door. Grandpapa, his voluminous cape only half on
and his top hat on one side, marched out of the house
and was heaved in by his panting butler; his black bag
of instruments was flung in after him, the door was
banged, Lebrun the coachman cracked his whip and the
du Frocq horses dashed off in hot pursuit of Dr.
Atkinson's inferior animals.

"Hurrah!" yelled the children.

"He's a sporting old boy, you know," Colin conceded, "though he is so d—er—pigheaded about
Albert."

"Don't swear, Colin," said Michelle with that elder-
sisterly primness which the others found so hard to
bear.

"Why not?" said Colin. "Grandpapa does. . . .
Now look here, girls, are we taking Albert this afternoon or are we not?"

They retired to the stable to consider the problem.

They sat in Albert's manger, and upon that animal's patient but uncommonly hard back, and argued hotly. They were on the whole obedient children but in this case some of them felt that they had a certain amount of justification for disobedience, because Grandpapa had behaved so extraordinarily badly. For one thing there was his hard-heartedness in denying to a child homesick for his mother the consolation of the donkey; and for another thing there was his injustice in complaining of their argumentativeness when absolutely no one had argued a single argue; and for a third thing he had dared to speak slightingly of their beloved mother.

"One doesn't have to obey tyrants like Nero and Grandpapa," said Peronelle at last with flashing eyes.

"Yet Mother said we were to," said Michelle.

"Let's toss for it," suggested Jacqueline.

"Tails take the donkey, heads not take the donkey," said Colin, and tossed.

It was take the donkey.... Grandpapa would never know because he always continued his rounds in the afternoon and would not be in when the picnic party started.

The old man was unusually chatty at lunch.

In the course of the morning he and Dr. Atkinson, both dashing in different directions after different patients, had collided at a street corner and both the dark-blue brougham and the dark-green brougham had suffered, but the dark-blue brougham had suffered most.

"Wrenched the fellow's right front wheel right off," triumphed Grandpapa, as though this was to his credit.

"How clever of you, Grandpapa," chorused his

grandchildren, but he was too absorbed in himself to notice the suspicious charm with which they spoke.

"Shan't be going out this afternoon," he continued, cheerfully masticating underdone roast beef.

"Not?" chorused the grandchildren faintly.

"No. Brougham out of action and weather too chilly for the dogcart. . . . Atkinson won't be going out this afternoon either with his brougham in the state it is."

"But he has a dogcart, too," piped Colette. "A beautiful dogcart, bigger than yours."

"What? What?" demanded Grandpapa, masticating Yorkshire pudding. "Nonsense. A cheap, rackety thing. The fellow's never seen in it if he can help it."

"You might both be suddenly sent for," suggested Michelle hopefully.

"What? What?" said Grandpapa, helping himself to his third roast potato. "Not likely. Too early in the year for strawberries and over-eating. . . . I'll take another piece of that Yorkshire pudding."

Half an hour later the children, armed with the picnic baskets and hats and coats, again sought the shelter of the stable to discuss the situation that had now arisen.

For the only possible way of getting Albert out to the road was along a cobbled lane that led under the library window, and in the library window sat Grandpapa, his newspaper on his knee, his silk handkerchief spread over his head and his hands folded over his waistcoat. It was true that his eyes were closed and that rhythmical snorts escaped from his well-shaped nostrils, but the sound of Albert's hoofs on the cobbles could not fail to awake him for, like all doctors, he always slept with one ear cocked.

"It's no good," said Michelle, "we must give it up."

"I'd sooner die!" flashed Peronelle.

"Let's carry Albert," said Colin.

"Yes!" they shrieked. "Good for you, Colin!"

"But what if he ee-haws?" asked Jacqueline, one of those tiresome people who always make difficulties.

"We'll tie his mouth up in Colette's flannel petti-coat," said Colin.

Colette was divested of her petticoat (a red one, scalloped) and this was done. Then Colin and Michelle took a front leg each and Peronelle and Jacqueline a back one. Colette was instructed to place herself in a stooping position underneath Albert, her back pressing upwards against him, in case Albert, who was stout, should sag in the middle and feel uncomfortable.

"Lift when I say three," said Peronelle. "Now then, you chaps. . . . One. Two. Three. . . . Help! Would you have believed he was so heavy?"

(A word should here be said, again in parenthesis, about Albert. He was, unlike most donkeys, an abso-lute angel. Indeed he was very like Colette in dis-position, combining as he did placidity and goodness with a certain roundness of form and fondness for the pleasures of the table; perhaps it was his likeness to her that made Grandpapa so fond of him. In colour he was a lovely pearl grey. His ears were long and silky and his nose, because he was not as young as he once had been, snow-white. Because of his years and his tendency to *embonpoint* he moved, as a rule, slowly and with dignity, but he could, when really roused, still go like the wind.)

"My stars! He must weigh a ton!" gasped Colin.

None of the others could speak. Straining, gasping, panting, staggering, they advanced inch by inch along the cobbled way. They came near the library window, they were level with it, they were past it, and then, suddenly, opening his jaws wide and bursting the seam of the flannel petticoat, Albert the Good ee-hawed.

The noise he made was incredible, considering the flannel petticoat. Off came the handkerchief from Grandpapa's head, down went his newspaper, up flew the library window and out came his head.

He made no comment at all. He merely adjusted his eyeglass and gazed, his face becoming congested and his throat swelling a little in his rage. The children lowered Albert to the ground, straightened their aching backs and panted silently, awaiting punishment.

When it came it fitted the crime.

"Pick up that donkey," said Grandpapa, "and take it back where it came from."

"What—carry it?" faltered Michelle.

"Yes, carry it," said Grandpapa. "If you carried it out you can carry it back. I shall be watching you from the window."

"Now then, you chaps," whispered Peronelle. "One. Two. Three."

They returned whence they had come, as they had come, Albert ee-hawing all the way.

．　　　．　　　．　　　．　　　．

"... TAKE IT BACK WHERE IT CAME FROM."

127

They lay flat on their backs on the stable floor, with dreadful pains in their insides after the strain of Albert's weight, and it was quite a long time before they felt better.

Peronelle felt better first.

"Colin," she said, sitting up, "go and see if Grandpapa is asleep again."

Colin, returning, said that he was. . . . Fast, with the newspaper as well as his handkerchief over his head.

"I thought so," said Peronelle. "Anger always sends him off. . . . Now's our chance."

"What for?" asked Jacqueline faintly.

"To carry Albert out again."

"We can't," moaned the others, "we'll die."

"How can man die better than in facing fearful odds?" demanded Peronelle. "Are you cowardly skunks to be ground beneath the heel of a tyrant or are you children of spirit?"

No du Frocq has ever been known, or ever will be known, to refuse the call to action. . . . Silently they arose from the floor.

Now Albert had by this time entered into the spirit of the game, or else he was getting used to things, or else he was simply tired, but anyhow he never ee-hawed. They reached the street half-dead but victorious.

About a mile or so out of the town of St. Pierre the delectable L'Ancre Common stretched from the rising ground where General Carew's big grey house was right down to the thundering waves of the Channel. It was covered with coarse grass and criss-crossed by low stone

128

walls where flowers grew, and down by the sea the sand-dunes were dotted with clumps of sea-holly. It was a lovely place to picnic for one could see for miles, the sun seemed to be always shining and the cloud shadows raced over the common like galloping horses.

Two roads crossed the common, the inland road that led past General Carew's house to some farms beyond and the coast road that passed through the little village of L'Ancre, a cluster of whitewashed houses down by the sea where the gardens were full of tamarisk trees and hedges of veronica. This coast road, when it had left L'Ancre behind, swerved inland and joined the other road just beyond General Carew's gate.

The children chose the inland road and tramped merrily along it, singing "Wrap me up in my Tarpaulin Jacket" and leading Albert with Colette and the food upon his back. They felt gloriously happy, for the sky was as blue as Colette's frock and the waves and the wind were singing too.

They felt happy, that is, until they suddenly rounded a bend in the road and saw in front of them a closed gate and a group of ragged little children standing by it. . . . They had quite forgotten the curse of L'Ancre Common —the highwaymen.

Every now and then, across both the roads, were closed gates that separated the grazing ground of one farmer from that of another, and it was the unpleasing habit of the Island ragamuffins to gather in clamorous groups at the gates and demand largesse. "*Des doubles, m'sieur et m'dame,*" they would yell when a carriage drew up at the gate. "*Des doubles! Des doubles!*" and unless satisfied they would leap upon the carriage step, frighten the horses and be as naughty as the sargousets, the Island goblins, themselves.

"There now!" cried Michelle. "Those wretched children! And we can't get over the wall because of Albert. . . . Has anybody any doubles?"

The Island had its own coinage in those days. Eight doubles made a penny, and a franc was tenpence, and the du Frocq children had only six doubles each a week as pocket-money, unless they liked to earn more by collecting snails in the garden. . . . It was a double for six snails.

Everyone's pockets were emptied but they could only scratch up six doubles between the lot of them.

"Why does Grandpapa never fork out anything except on birthdays?" demanded Colin savagely. "He's a mean, stingy old miser. Any decent grandparent would chuck a few doubles about the place now and again. . . . Or a franc piece. . . . He wouldn't miss it."

Colin had reason for his strong feelings for four out of the six doubles were his, for snails, and there is nothing of which one hates to be robbed more than hard-won earnings.

"Cheer up," comforted Jacqueline. "I bet you Grandpapa will tip us before we leave."

"Not he!" snorted Colin. "I bet you anything you like to mention he won't cough up anything at all. . . . Not after Albert."

"Done," said Jacqueline promptly. "Your mummied frog against my bottled snake."

"Done," said Colin.

They reached the gate and instantly the highwaymen were all round them; bright-eyed little rascals with skin tanned a rich brown by the sun, bare legs and feet and bright-hued, ragged clothes. "*Des doubles, m'sieur et m'dames!*" they yelled. "*Des doubles! Des doubles!*"

"Little beasts!" said Colin through his teeth. . . . They did not understand English very well so one could say what one liked.

"Now behave decently, you children," said Michelle to her brother and sisters in her most irritating manner. "If one gives at all one should give with a smile."

"Hold your tongue, Michelle!" said Peronelle. "None of the six doubles are yours, remember, they're Colin's and mine, and it's us to say if we're going to behave well or not, not you."

However it was not in the nature of a du Frocq not to be generous and the six doubles were handed over to the highwaymen with a good grace, together with a rather stale piece of cake that no one fancied.

The highwaymen, however, were not satisfied, and refused to open the gate. "*Pas beaucoup*," they said, and spat.

"You're disgusting, greedy little children," said Peronelle loftily. "We have given you our all and you spit. . . . Turn out your pockets, you others."

All the du Frocq pockets were turned out, displaying grubby handkerchiefs and Colin's mummied frog, but nothing else. The highwaymen, appeased, grinned disarmingly—they really were enchanting children— their white teeth flashing in their brown faces. "*Bon *jour, m'sieur et m'dames,"* they said. "*Dieu vous garde.*"

It is nice to be blest, especially by the poor, and it makes one feel good to be generous, even though one was forced to be, so the children's faces wore expressions of smug satisfaction as they sat eating their tea in a sandy hollow between the two roads.

From where they were they could see the whole landscape. To their right was the town of St. Pierre clinging to its rocky cliff, to their left, down by the sea, the village of L'Ancre, while behind them, sheltered by a clump of storm-twisted trees, was General Carew's house.

When they had eaten everything there was to eat they lay in a happy, tired heap blinking at the sun, while Albert the Good cropped the grass and wild thyme and enjoyed himself.

So contented were they that they were half asleep when an unmistakable sound made them suddenly sit bolt upright. . . . Clip-clop, clip-clop. . . . The sound of a horse's hoofs came faintly through the singing of the wind in the grasses and the surging of the waves. Five heads were turned anxiously towards the coast road and there, sure enough, was Grandpapa's yellow dogcart bowling along in the direction of L'Ancre, and Grandpapa himself sitting up beside Lebrun in his tall top hat.

"Heaven help us!" moaned Michelle. "Someone's been taken suddenly ill at L'Ancre. . . . Can he see Albert from there?"

"Down, Albert, down!" hissed the others, and hurried the unfortunate donkey behind a sand-dune.

And then, swift and inevitable as the events in a Greek tragedy, it all happened.

"Look!" cried Jacqueline, and pointed an excited finger at General Carew's house. A maidservant had come out of it and was running wildly towards them, stumbling over the tussocks of grass, the white streamers of her smart cap flying out behind her.

She crossed the first road and came to the children. "The doctor!" she gasped. "I saw him from the window. That's the doctor's dogcart!" and tripping over a tuft of sea-holly she fell headlong.

"Yes," said the children, heaving her up. "Dr. du Frocq. Do you want him?"

"The General!" gasped the distracted girl. "His apoplexy! *Mon Dieu*, I've lost my breath! One of you children run."

Needless to say they all ran; Albert, who hated being lonely, following heavily in the rear.

They came up with Grandpapa on the outskirts of L'Ancre but unfortunately they had reckoned without the nerves of Victoria, Grandpapa's mare, who was a very temperamental lady indeed.

Finding herself charged by five children and a donkey, and seeing a creature with alarming white streamers growing out of the back of her head not far behind, Victoria shied and plunged, tried to recover herself, lost her footing again and fell heavily to her knees. Had not Grandpapa and Lebrun both been stout and heavily cloaked, and so wedged firmly into the front

133

seat, they would have flown over Victoria's head. As it was Grandpapa had a good deal to say.

"But the General, Grandpapa!" cried Peronelle, interrupting his flow of language. "He has the apoplexy. Hurry! Hurry!"

"What? What?" cried Grandpapa, and he lifted his head like an old war horse going into action; as was his habit when any indisposition threatened a Carew.

"Yes, monsieur, if you please," cried the maid, coming panting up to them. "The General's very bad!"

"Drive on, Lebrun!" commanded Grandpapa in ringing professional tones. "Never mind about the woman at L'Ancre. . . . She can wait. . . . General Carew's."

But Victoria was not going to be driven on. She had broken both her knees, was in the throes of a nerve-storm and had no intention of going anywhere except home. She rolled her eyes, foamed at the mouth, kicked and vowed that her back was broken.

"No good, monsieur," moaned Lebrun. "You know what she is."

Grandpapa knew and descended hastily and heavily from his seat, grasping his black bag and growling horribly. . . . He must walk, and he hated walking.

"Never mind, darling Grandpapa," piped Colette. "Let the other doctor go," and she pointed a fat finger in the direction of the inland road.

Eight pairs of eyes—no, ten, for Victoria and Albert looked too—followed her pointing finger and beheld a smart scarlet dogcart bowling along in the direction of the farms. . . . Dr. Atkinson's dogcart, and he was not very far from General Carew's door.

"Thank the good God! The English doctor!" gasped the maid, and was gone like an arrow from a bow.

Colette, of course, was too young to understand that the honour of the du Frocqs was at stake, but the other four understood only too well. Their eyes flew in an agony of affection to Grandpapa's flushed and furious face and they had every sympathy with the language he was using. . . . For though, like all high-spirited families, the du Frocqs did not always see eye to eye, yet at bottom they loved each other and in times of trouble they always showed a united front against the enemy. . . . At this awful moment the children simply adored Grandpapa; and Peronelle's love instantly took the form of practical action.

"Albert!" she cried. "Get on Albert!"

Before Grandpapa knew what was happening he found himself taken charge of by his descendants. He was on his beloved donkey, he found, and bumping along at an incredible pace. He shouted to the children to stop, for he felt the indignity of his position very strongly, but they took no more notice of his forcible language than they would have taken of the buzzing of a bluebottle. Peronelle rushed on ahead, dragging Albert by his reins, Michelle and Jacqueline scampered on each side and Colin, armed with a stick, urged on Albert from behind, all of them shouting like young furies.

135

"Go on, Albert!" they yelled. "Good old Albert! Albert the Good forever!"

And Albert, in spite of his age and weight, galloped like mad; he laid his ears back, rolled his eyes and simply pounded. Whether he really knew what was expected of him, or whether he wanted to show Victoria that he could do better than she could any day, or whether he was terrified and was running away no one knew, but anyhow he went like the wind.

It was a near thing, and a grand race, for Grandpapa on the coast road and Dr. Atkinson on the inland road were about equidistant from the General's front gate.

Out of the tail of an agonized eye Peronelle saw that wretched maid reach the scarlet dogcart, saw it draw up and saw Dr. Atkinson bend down to hear what she had to say. Then he straightened himself, leaned forward and laid his whip across his horse's back; and his horse was a fine horse and a willing one. . . . Now it's all up, moaned Peronelle to herself, for poor old Albert can't go like that. . . . Perspiration dripped down her forehead and furious tears brimmed over and rolled down her cheeks, but in spite of her despair she did not give up, she ran faster than ever and behind her she could hear the shouts of the others increasing in hoarseness and desperation.

"Stop, you young rascals, stop!" roared Grandpapa, but he was not listened to.

And then Peronelle, her eyes momentarily clear of tears, saw something that she had not noticed before; a second gate across the road between Dr. Atkinson and his objective, and running towards it the very same young highwaymen who had robbed them before tea at the first gate. . . . They had probably robbed Dr. Atkinson at the first gate, too, so they must be making this second attempt simply because they had grasped the situation and had a sporting spirit. . . . Were they going to be little sports? . . . Were they?

A mist once more obscured her vision but a wild shout of triumph from Colin told her that they were. Then her sight cleared and she saw Dr. Atkinson reining in his plunging horse while the crowd of ragamuffins swarmed over the gate and climbed upon the step of his dogcart. *"Des doubles, m'sieur, des doubles, des doubles!"* came their shrill voices on the wind.

That hold-up finished Dr. Atkinson and five minutes later the du Frocq cavalcade galloped in through the General's garden gate.

That evening, by Grandpapa's invitation, the children joined him at dessert, dressed in their best, and found him in magnificent spirits. He gathered them round him, gave them an apple each, chucked them under their chins and told them what he said to the dentist the first time he had a tooth out; the relating of which anecdote was a sure sign of good humour with him and up till now had taken place only on Christmas Day and Easter Day. Colette he took upon his knee so that he could poke his finger through her curls and comfort her with sugared figs. . . . For Colette was a little sad. . . . Owing to her tender years and her weight she had not been able to keep up in the great race, though she had tried hard, and she had been obliged

I   137

to return to Lebrun and Victoria. But she felt much better after the figs and smiled very sweetly as she lay munching with her head on her relative's starched shirt-front.

Grandpapa's good humour was justified, for only a couple of hours before the General had said to him faintly: "You've saved my life, Doctor, you've saved my life," and had weakly but warmly pressed his hand; and as every lightest word spoken by a Carew was always all over the Island by nine o'clock the next morning this meant that Grandpapa and the *status quo* were established for ever.... That fool Atkinson, with his ridiculous modern ideas and his chitter-chatter about antiseptics and sucklike tomfoolery was now nowhere, simply nowhere.... Grandpapa polished his eyeglass, adjusted it, and beamed upon Peronelle. ... How well she had organized the whole affair.... And Michelle.... She might be plain but he liked her spirit.... And Jacqueline and Colin.... How those two could shout.... All the dear children, he thought, had behaved uncommonly well. What? What? Yes, uncommonly well, and he'd go so far as to say so to their mother on her return.

"Don't you think we ought to go and say good night to Albert?" asked Peronelle, when Colette could eat no more. "After all, we owe everything to Albert."

Grandpapa was in a mood to agree to everything, even though the hour was late and chilly, so they trooped out to the stable, collecting some carrots and a banana—Albert was partial to bananas—from the kitchen on their way.

Picnic With Albert

Albert was refreshing himself at his manger when they came in and was not interested in them until he suddenly saw the banana out of the tail of his eye, when he turned round and reached for it greedily, but seemed anxious not to let the children come too close. . . . His reluctance to allow them near his legs suddenly reminded Grandpapa of the occurrences of the early afternoon.

"How the blazes," he demanded, "did you get that donkey out again?"

"Carried him," they said.

"What? What? A third time?"

"Yes," they said.

Grandpapa was without words, and his face became so congested that the children feared another explosion, but he was only speechless from admiration. . . . The energy, he thought, the determination of these young rascals. . . . It was easy to see whom they took after. . . . They were his very own grandchildren. . . . He plunged his left hand into his pocket, brought up a handful of loose change and gave them two francs each all round.

Silently Colin plunged his right hand into *his* pocket and producing his mummied frog he handed it to Jacqueline with a bow.

Chapter Six

DOING GOOD

In the autumn of 1891, when Colette and Colin du Frocq were aged respectively eight and eleven years old, they had mumps. Eighteen ninety-one was ever afterwards referred to by Rachell, their mother, as "the frightful mumps year." Not that the mumps in itself was frightful; it was not; Colette and Colin suffered the affliction in its mildest form and their exuberant spirits and excellent health seemed quite unimpaired, but in their swollen condition they could not go to church with the rest of the family on Sundays, but remained at home to be taught scripture by Rachell, and the consequences of her religious teaching were quite dreadful.

She didn't know why. All she did was to tell them Bible stories, explaining the meaning and pointing the moral to the best of her ability, and they promptly went out and did appalling things, doing them moreover as a result of her teaching and in a truly Christian spirit. . . . On the final mumps Sunday Rachell came to the conclusion that if there is anything more dangerous to property than vice it is morality.

And yet it was her own fault. So vivid was her imagination that a story re-told by her put on so many frills and embroideries in the re-telling that it was scarcely recognizable in its original form. She was one of those, of whom the world is not worthy, who delight to leave a story better than they find it. She did this with the story of the Good Samaritan on the last Sunday of September, 1891, and the consequences were with her for years.

The three of them sat together, that Sunday morning, in the parlour of the old farmhouse of Bon Repos. Pools of sunshine lay on the floor and the room was very still. There seemed no sound in all the world but Rachell's lovely voice, flowing on like a song, and the distant accompaniment of the murmuring sea. . . . For Bon Repos was the loveliest house in the loveliest island of the Channel Islands and the sound of the sea accompanied every thought and word and action from its birth to its death, so constant a friend that it was hardly noticed.

The room where they sat was very old and very lovely, and the china and furniture that lived in it lived there because they were beautiful and because Rachell was a woman who knew how to match a jewel with its setting.

She herself was a jewel and so, in their different ways, were Colette and Colin. Rachell was a tall, stately woman with a glorious crown of dark hair and warm, compassionate eyes. She sat now in a low chair, the folds of her black Sunday silk billowing round her and the cameo brooch in the bosom of her dress rising and falling with every soft movement of her breast. Her beautiful, shapely hands held her open Bible but, carried away by her own eloquence as she was, she entirely neglected to verify the statements that she made, an omission that she afterwards regretted.

In front of her, on two footstools, their eyes fixed on her face, sat her offspring. Colette in her white Sunday starched muslin, with her golden curls and her amber eyes, was a rather substantial symphony in white and gold. For Colette was on the stout side. In the years to come, when her lover put his arms about her and strained her to his bosom—and who could doubt that anything so adorable as Colette would have a lover— he would have a decided armful and there would be something considerable to strain. Colin in his white sailor suit was a complete contrast to his sister. He was slender and dark and vividly alive and had quick, bird-like movements that contrasted amusingly with Colette's stately perambulations, so reminiscent of Queen Victoria at the less slender periods of her illustrious life. They both of them looked extremely devout but in the case of Colin this was an illusion only.

"I am going to tell you the story of the Good Samaritan," said Rachell earnestly.

"What did he have for breakfast?" interrupted Colin.

"Eggs," said Rachell, never at a loss for an answer.

"How many?" asked Colette, whose appetite was enormous and who always secretly hankered after several eggs for her breakfast instead of the regulation one.

"Three," said Rachell, who had always imagined the Good Samaritan as one of those large, benevolent men who need a lot of nourishment.

Doing Good

"Then he was *not* good," said Colin, "he was greedy. When I said to you last Wednesday, 'Mother, may I have another egg?' you said, 'Don't be greedy, Colin.'"

"Ah, but he didn't eat the eggs," said Rachell hastily. "Just as he was going to crack the top off the first one he looked out of the window and saw a poor, hungry little boy, and he picked up his breakfast, the eggs and the toast and everything, and took it out to the poor little boy."

"Didn't he have *any* breakfast, then?" asked Colin.

"No, he was so good that he gave it all away."

"What a giddy goat," said Colin, to whose practical nature the extravagant charity of the elect made no appeal, and his attention wandered to the worms he was harbouring in his pocket until his religious duties were over and he could go and fish in the pond.

But Colette, who had a beautiful, saintly disposition, had taken the incident of the eggs very much to heart. She leant forward, her eyes wide and absorbed, her expression that of one of Reynolds' fat-necked cherubs. "Mother," she said, "did he give away *all* the eggs?"

"Yes, darling."

"Didn't he keep even one for himself?"

"No, he gave them all."

"Then, Mother, oughtn't we to give away things that we have to poor people?"

Rachell hastened to improve the shining moment. "Yes, darling, of course we ought. It says so in the Bible again and again."

"And we ought to give all? Like the Good Samaritan and the widow with her mite?"

"Er—yes, darling," said Rachell, with only the slightest hesitation. . . . Really, it was impossible to explain to children that if we all took the Bible quite literally in the nineteenth century the State would be quite unable to support the number of workhouses that would be required.

"What's a mite?" asked Colin. "I thought it was a kind of little worm that lived in cheese."

"I think we had better go on with the story now," said Rachell, who felt that they were running off the rails even before they could be said to have got firmly on them. "Well, when the Good Samaritan had finished his breakfast——"

"But he didn't have any," interrupted Colin.

"No more he did. Well, anyway, he was going on a long journey, so he saddled his ass——"

"Where was he going to?" asked Colette. "Was he going to see his father and mother?"

"Yes, darling, but don't interrupt. . . . And he put on his beautiful, best striped cloak——"

"Did he wear wool next his skin?" asked Colin.

"Children," said Rachell, "I think you must be quite quiet while I tell you this story."

There was a note in her voice that they knew and respected and they said not one word more, indeed after two minutes they did not want to, for the story enthralled them. Such a clear painter of word pictures was Rachell that they saw it all. They saw the Good Samaritan, clothed in his best blue cloak with the yellow stripes and with a turban thing on his head, jogging along the white, dusty road on his ass, with a hot, blue sky arching over his head and the dust giving him a tickle in the throat. They saw him give a little start as he saw a huddled object lying at the side of the road on ahead of him. At first he thought it was a man but then he knew it couldn't be because another man on ahead of him, when he saw the huddled object, only passed by on the other side. It must be a dead animal, the Good Samaritan probably thought, and it must be very dead indeed or the other man wouldn't have put himself to all the trouble of passing by on the other side. But when he got up to the huddled object it was a man, a poor creature who had been set upon and robbed and hurt most dreadfully. The Good Samaritan was so angry with the man who had passed by on the other side that he went beetroot in the face with rage, and jumping off his ass he hurried to the poor wounded man and asked him gently if it hurt, and if so, where? The wounded man said it did hurt, and everywhere, and he was thirsty, so the Good Samaritan gave him his water-bottle to drink from and let him have the very last drop, even though his own throat was tickling more and more with the dust, and he lifted him on his own ass and took him to an inn and looked after him, binding up his wounds and pouring in oil and wine to make them better. Colette and Colin could see it all, they could smell the blood soaking into the dust and feel how lovely and cool the water was to the poor man's throat, and the oil and wine, even though the remedy seemed odd for wounds, they felt to be doubtless very soothing.

The story affected them both differently. To Colin's adventurous disposition it was a glorious idea for a game; to Colette's pious one it was an example of benevolence that must immediately be followed. But they both wanted to know the end and felt the one provided by Holy Writ to be most unsatisfactory, entirely neglecting, as it did, even to indicate the future history either of the Good Samaritan or of the poor wounded man. Did he get quite well afterwards, Colette wanted to know, and were the Good Samaritan's father and mother pleased to see him, and were they all happy ever afterwards? She got so tearful about the uncertainty of the whole thing that Rachell hastened to comfort her. Yes, she said, the Good Samaritan's father and mother were very pleased to see him, and when the poor wounded man got quite well the Good Samaritan fetched him to live with the father and mother and look after their pigs, and everybody, including the pigs, lived happy ever after.

At the midday family dinner Colette was very silent, her jaws champing up and down busily and her mind occupied, not for the first time, with the extraordinary inconsistency of grown-ups. Her mother had that morning told her, quite definitely, that one should give away all that one had to the poor, and yet here they all were, her father and mother, her three elder sisters, herself and Colin, gobbling up roast mutton and onion sauce, with apple tart to follow, and apparently giving not one thought to the poor. It was all very puzzling and Colette heaved a great sigh, caused partly by repletion and partly by the disturbed condition of her mind.

Colin, too, was wondering a little at the curious habits

of his elders. The conversation, to which Colette was paying no attention, had turned upon some poor fisherman's boy who lived down at Breton Bay, a hamlet only a short way from Bon Repos. He had been left an orphan, it appeared, and the uncle and aunt who had taken him in treated him shamefully.

"Sophie says they beat him," said Michelle, the eldest du Frocq, retailing the gossip of an old servant. "And they don't give him enough to eat. The child's becoming quite an idiot through ill treatment."

"Beasts!" said Peronelle, the second du Frocq, scarlet with indignation. "Why doesn't someone do something about it? Could I have some more tart, please, Mother?"

"Someone should adopt the poor child," said Rachell.

"Cases like that ought to be seen to," pronounced André, her husband.

So like grown-ups, thought Colin. Always saying that so-and-so should be done but never doing it themselves. It exasperated him. Not that he felt any particular pity for the little boy, for never having seen misery in any form, pity was not as yet a part of his make-up, but statements that were not at once followed by vigorous action seemed to him useless and stupid. He himself, if he said he was going to put his pet rat in a sister's bed, immediately put his pet rat in a sister's bed, and braved the consequences. Inaction and hesitation in any form infuriated him, as they did Peronelle. . . . For a second their eyes met, both pairs ablaze with indignation, and something unseen, but important in its consequences, passed between them.

After dinner, as always on a Sunday afternoon, they made a tour of inspection. The farm did not do too badly, for André du Frocq had lately been left sufficient money by a brother to pay a competent bailiff to be a better farmer than he was himself. He meanwhile, comfortably removed from the burden and heat of the day, was a poet and a philosopher, one of those who inform a world not removed from the burden and heat of the day that life is good. . . . He was not, perhaps, always believed, but in his chosen vocation he was a happy man.

They looked at the well-stocked garden and the fat pigs and the sleek cows and the fussy hens and, last of all, they looked at their apples. Most of the orchards on the Island that year had failed to bear, and the du Frocq orchard had also not done its duty, but one particular apple tree had borne nobly. Lovely, russet-brown apples tinged with scarlet lay in luscious rows in the apple-room.

"Aren't they lovely?" breathed Michelle.

"We must be careful of them," said Rachell, almost reverently. "They must last till Christmas. . . . André, let's go in."

The family separated, Rachell and André for their Sunday siesta in the parlour, the three elder girls to read in the kitchen and Colette and Colin to play in the garden.

"You're not to go out, children," was Rachell's parting remark. "You must promise me to stay in the garden."

"Promise," said Colette.

"Darling Mother," said Colin, not committing himself.

Rachell, satisfied, left them.

They trotted round the house to the kitchen garden behind, so as to be beyond the prying eyes of their sisters.

"Let's play at being the Good Samaritan," said Colin, "and you can be the ass."

But Colette shook her yellow curls. "Not if it's upstairs," she said. She had eaten a very large dinner and she was feeling her weight. What she wanted to do for the present was to sit quietly in a fat heap at the end of the garden and just wonder about things.

"Lazy little cabbage," said Colin scornfully, and left her.

Colette did not mind being scorned, the very good frequently are, and she was used to it. She ran down to the bottom of the garden, where beautiful umbrellas of rhubarb sprouted beside the gate that led on to the road. This was one of her favourite spots for wondering but to-day she had not time to wonder a single wonder, for peeping through the bars of the gate was a little, dirty boy. His face was thin, and furrowed by tear marks running through grime, and his dark eyes were the eyes of a rabbit caught in a trap. His jersey was torn and his toes were coming through his boots.

Colette's heart seemed to turn right over. She had a compassionate heart and it not infrequently performed these somersaults but, unlike most hearts, when it turned right way up again it immediately goaded her into action. In the twinkling of an eye she had taken off her best strap shoes and thrust them through the bars at the little boy.... He remained tepid.... "I'd rather have something to eat, Mamselle," he muttered hoarsely.

Not a bit discouraged Colette restored the shoes to her feet and sped into the house to the larder. . . . But Rachell, remembering the attacks of hunger that sometimes seized Colin in the middle of a Sunday afternoon, had locked the larder. . . . For a moment Colette was near tears and then she suddenly remembered the apples. "They must last till Christmas," Rachell had said, but then she had also said, "We must give away all that we have to the poor," and the only thing to be done with the conflicting commands of grown-ups was to obey the one that seemed most applicable at the moment. . . . She sped to the apple-room.

"How many would you like?" she asked, returning with a pinafore full.

"How many have you got?" he asked.

"There's a sackful there," puffed Colette.

"Then could I have the sackful, Mamselle?" he breathed earnestly.

"Could you eat all that?" asked Colette, overcome with admiration for a feat of appetite that even surpassed anything of her own.

"No, Mamselle, but I could sell them." He leaned nearer to her, trembling all over, his face white beneath its grime. "If I could buy myself tidy clothes I could get work. . . . Like this they would not take me."

AT THE END OF TEN MINUTES THE SACK WAS FULL

Colette, looking at his rags, agreed that perhaps they wouldn't.

"Come with me to get the apples," she whispered.

"I daren't," he said.

Something of his animal fear and trembling haste passed into Colette. She made three journeys to the apple-room and back, bouncing along at a pace that was not in the least reminiscent of Queen Victoria, and at the end of ten minutes the sack was full and on his back and he was staggering off down the road, panting with eagerness and not even waiting to say thank-you. . . . Not that she minded. She always gave for the sake of the person to whom she gave and with no thought of herself.

Turning back from the gate, flushed with benevolence, she found herself face to face with Colin, who was coming down the path attired in Peronelle's new striped silk dressing-gown, with a towel twisted turbanwise round his head and his dog Maximilian attached to his person by a rope. In one hand he held a bottle of cod liver oil and in the other a bottle of turpentine.

"I'm the Good Samaritan," he announced, "and Maximilian is the ass since you wouldn't be."

"What's the cod liver oil and the turpentine for?" asked Colette.

"The oil and the wine to pour into the wounds," he said, and hitching up his dressing-gown he opened the gate.

"You mustn't go out," remonstrated Colette. "Mother said not to."

"I didn't promise not to, I wasn't such a giddy goat,

I just said, 'Darling Mother,' and left it at that."

Colin stalked out of the gate and down the road. . . . Colette watched him, green with envy. She would have liked to go too but already, young as she was, she was terribly handicapped by an active conscience, and duty kept her tethered.

Colin trudged down the white, dusty road beneath the hot, blue sky of Palestine, his noble ass lolloping behind. The sun scorched him and the dust tickled his throat and the dressing-gown was distinctly hot, but he did not mind these things because he was good, and nothing, in stories that is, ever upsets the good.

Presently, the heat of the sun being what it was, he turned to the right and plunged down a leafy lane. There was nothing in the story about the Good Samaritan turning sideways but one might as well be comfortable as not. At the bottom of this first lane he turned to the left into a second, a lovely lane with a stream running down it. This was a short cut to the town and was very well known to Colin, whose private business frequently took him townwards unknown to his parents, yet to-day, his own character being changed, the character of the lane was changed, too. It was not an Island lane any longer, it was a dusty track crossing the treeless fields of the Holy Land, and at any moment now he might come upon that prostrate figure by the roadside. . . . Already he could smell the blood soaking into the dust. . . . He jerked the rope to accelerate the movements of the ass and took a firmer grip on the bottle of cod liver oil.

Therefore it was a distinct surprise, when he turned a corner, to come face to face with not one prostrate figure but four. Four boys were kicking and sprawling and cursing together in the middle of the path, a confused mass of arms and legs and shouts, and all round them rolled russet-brown apples tinged with scarlet. For a moment Colin stood still, nonplussed, for the thing was not working out according to plan. Then he realized what had happened. The Good Samaritan had arrived upon the scene a shade too soon and the thieves were caught in the act. All the better. With a yell of triumph he flung the dressing-gown from him into the stream and rushed to the rescue. The noble ass, showing all his teeth and brandishing his tail like a banner of war, leapt into the fight, too, and instantly there began such a bloody battle as the water lane has not seen before or since. Colin was a magnificent fighter, second to none, and Colette's little dirty boy fought with the courage of desperation and the others with the courage of greed. They all five—six, counting Maximilian—bit and scratched and punched and kicked with incomparable vigour, while the sun and moon and stars stood still to watch, and victory, as always in Holy Writ, went to the righteous. The robbers were vanquished at last and fled home to their mothers in a pitiable state. . . . But not before they had somehow succeeded in gathering up most of the apples.

The Good Samaritan and the poor wounded man sat up and looked at each other. The story was now progressing along the proper lines except that the Good

Samaritan was rather the worse wounded of the two. One of his eyes was closed up and his nose was bleeding, and he had a horrid cut on his cheek given him by the bottle of turpentine, which had had the bad taste to get itself smashed in the middle of the mêlée. The bottle of cod liver oil had not smashed, but the cork had come out, and it had emptied itself in a slimy mess all over Maximilian.

"They *were* thieves all right, weren't they?" demanded Colin, his one eye sparkling with interest.

"Trying to steal my apples they were," growled the wounded man, and swore. "I'll kill 'em, so I will, when next I catch 'em."

Colin cast his eye upon the few bruised apples that were left. . . . Russet and scarlet. . . . Nowhere but at Bon Repos did one see such apples. . . . He leapt to his feet.

"Thief!" he yelled. "You stole those from Bon Repos. Thief! Thief! *Sal petit cochon!*"

At this dreadful Island insult the wounded man also leapt to his feet. "Liar!" he shouted. "Liar! I didn't steal 'em!"

Out shot their fists and the whole thing began all over again. Backwards and forwards they swayed, pommelling and thumping, Maximilian prancing round and barking ecstatically. Then with a thud they came down on the path, the Good Samaritan gloriously on top. . . . With the courtesy of the victor he instantly removed himself and assisted the vanquished to sit up.

"What's your name?" he demanded.

"Pierre," growled the wounded one.

Colin wiped blood out of his eye and had a good look. In the final scuffle Pierre's jersey had been completely torn off him, and Colin saw a bony back with long weals across it. . . . He had never seen such a thing before and he felt suddenly sick. . . . Then he remembered the conversation at dinner and gripped Pierre's arm.

"Are you the boy who lives at Breton Bay and whose uncle beats him?" he demanded.

Pierre nodded indifferently. "I didn't steal those apples, M'sieur," he pleaded. "The mamselle at Bon Repos gave them to me."

"Which mamselle?" asked Colin.

"The nice fat little one."

The description was adequate and Colin believed him and nodded. Then he sat back on his heels wondering what to do next. What with his eye and his nose and his bruises he felt a little heavy and confused, and the sight of the weals on Pierre's back had done something to him. For the first time in his life he was over-whelmed by pity, a sensation apparently situated in the pit of the stomach, and it made him feel quite queer. In its confusion his mind went groping back to the story he was acting and instantly light dawned. The wounded man had been taken by the Good Samaritan to live with his father and mother and look after the pigs. . . . A good deal had taken place first, but the story was now being re-enacted in a compressed form and there wasn't time for everything. . . . "Come on," he said to Pierre, and dragged him to his feet.

When the family assembled in the kitchen for tea

Colin was not there, but as all the attention was focused upon Colette his absence was hardly noticed.

Colette's disposition was the very reverse of secretive, and at each meal it was usually her habit to tell everyone exactly what she had done since she last took nourishment. She recounted the afternoon's adventure with placidity and a certainty of approval, touching lightly upon her mother's remarks of the morning and dwelling at length upon the hunger of the little boy. If the silence that followed her narration was ominous she was too much occupied in not biting over the jam in the middle of her doughnut to notice it.

Rachell, with the ease of long practice, recovered quickly from the shock and silenced the outcry of the rest of the family with a swift look. "*All* the apples, darling?" she asked faintly.

"All," said Colette. "You said this morning one must give all," and she gave a little crow of pleasure as she found the jam and bit deep into it.

"Is it better for the community at large that the young should be instructed in the rudiments of religion by their mothers or by Holy Church?" asked André mildly, but no one answered him, for Colin and Pierre had appeared in the doorway.

At the sight of her son's torn and blood-stained garments Rachell nearly fainted, but then she perceived the bloom of health on his cheek, recovered, and arose in her wrath.

"Colin, what on earth have you been doing?" she demanded. "And who is this little boy?"

"He's Pierre," said Colin, "and he's come to live

157

with us. I've told him he's to live with us and he says
he'd like to. . . . He's the wounded man and I'm the
Good Samaritan."

Rachell swayed where she stood. "Peronelle," she
said, "take them away and wash them."

Peronelle the practical was already on her feet, and
had haled them upstairs in the twinkling of an eye, but
in twenty minutes she was back again, her lovely face
glowing with eagerness.

"Mother!" she cried, "it *is* the little boy!"

"What little boy?" asked Rachell weakly.

"The one Sophie told us about. The one you said
someone should adopt. And Father said cases like that
ought to be seen to."

"By the parish," said André hastily.

"The parish!" cried Peronelle scornfully. "The
parish indeed! Think of Oliver Twist. A child like
that wants love and he is going to get it. I've told him
he shall stay with us. He's a darling. He shall be
our boot-boy and help in the garden and with the pigs."

"Peronelle, is this my house or yours?" demanded
Rachell, enraged. "I tell you I will not have it turned
into a workhouse without my permission. You
children have already made me take on the most in-
competent maidservant ever endured, simply as an act
of charity, and I cannot and will not have a second of
the species about the place. . . . It's too much. . . .
It's simply too much." Her lovely eyes, full of angry
tears, sought her husband's. "André, for pity's sake
go and deal with it."

André looked up and cleared his throat deprecatingly.

This, his children knew, was a sure sign that he was about to do as he was told, and Peronelle flew round the table and wound her arms round his neck.

"Keep him, Father," she whispered into his left ear, "keep him!" Her arms round him were trembling and her cheek against his was hot. . . . A tear fell and trickled down his neck. . . . Caught as he was between the devil and the deep sea of two lovely, determined women, and both of them his, he capitulated to the one whose arms were round his neck.

"I think, dear," he said to his wife, "that since all this is the result of your own religious teaching——"

"Very well," said Rachell, her eyes blazing. "You are of course master in your own house."

This was a statement that she frequently made in moments of wrath and André, who wasn't, often wondered if she really believed it.

"Yes, dear," he said gently, "and I should like the little boy to stay."

It was the first time he had ever won a victory over her and from then on there was almost a martial note in his poems.

But by night Rachell's sense of humour had come to the rescue and she was ashamed of herself. . . . Also Peronelle had shown her the scars on Pierre's back and she had cried for pity.

"Poor little soul!" she said to André, as she stood in front of her looking-glass brushing out her long hair for the night. "I'm so glad, darling, that you gave in to me and decided to keep him after all."

André, who was sitting up in the four-poster reading a book, started slightly and then smiled.

"Yes, dear," he said sweetly, "I am glad, too. I am always glad when your romantic heart triumphs over my more practical one."

His wife looked at him affectionately. He looked so funny sitting up in bed in his white nightshirt, rather like a gnome with his grey beard and ruffled hair and his spectacles on the end of his nose. She wondered if the people who read his beautiful poems pictured him as an exquisite young man in a black velvet coat with a lily in his buttonhole. They would, perhaps, get a shock if they saw him, but she herself preferred him as he was. She was much blessed in her husband, she considered, and sometimes, but not always, in her children.

"Those young wretches!" she sighed. "All my apples gone and my house turned into an orphanage without my leave. . . . If I have any more children, André, I shall bring them up heathens."

André glanced up over his spectacles. "I think, dear," he said, "that in teaching religion to children emphasis should be laid on those stories that encourage reverence for parental property."

Rachell, her hair-brush raised, paused. "Are there any?" she asked.

Chapter Seven

THE FORESTERS' RIDE

FEW grown-up people like the season of autumn. Winter is coming with its cold winds and rheumatism, its sleet and influenza, its lowered vitality and the cost of coal; their hearts fail within them; but to the children, who think of none of these things, it is of all seasons the most magical. Especially in the Channel Islands, and especially to the du Frocq children.

For, young demons though they were, they had eyes and ears for beauty. They liked the tawny bracken and fading purple heather that covered the cliffs, and the splendour of the high autumn tides that dashed in over the rocks below. They liked the smell of wood-smoke and the sad autumn crying of the gulls. They liked the blackberries and sloes and nuts in the hedges and the golden rain of the falling leaves. They liked the great turning wings of M'sieur Bougourd's windmill on windy days, the high white clouds racing in from the sea and the thought that the fifth of November was not far off.

Guy Fawkes' Day is the children's autumn festival. It is the last blaze of riot and colour before the winter rains damp down the fires of autumn. There will not be such laughter again until the candles are lit on the Christmas tree and the yule-log flames on the hearth.

On the Island, the Islanders being all children at heart, it was everybody's festival. The children had it all their own way earlier in the day when, shouting and singing joyously, they propelled their guys in wooden boxes on wheels up and down the steep twisting streets of the town of St. Pierre, and through the narrow lanes that linked hamlet to hamlet and farm to farm.

> "Please to remember
> The Fifth of November,
> Gunpowder treason and plot.
> I see no reason
> Why gunpowder treason
> Should ever be forgot."

So they sang to let folk know they were coming, and then demanded "*Des doubles! Des sous!*" in shrill voices that would not be hushed until they were satisfied. But when dark fell the grown-ups came into their own. It was the fathers and mothers who lit fireworks in backyards for their shrieking offspring, and it was the men of the Island, the fishermen and farmers, and anyone else who liked to join them, who galloped on horseback round the Island in that mad, gay adventure known as "the Foresters' Ride."

Part of the Island, once thickly wooded, was known as the Forest, and it was the Forest men who had first instituted this particular form of highway robbery. Clothed in the maddest, gayest clothes they could find,

with knots of ribbon pinned in their hats and coloured
scarves knotted round their throats, with their faces
blacked with burnt cork, carrying flaming torches and
mounted on whatever four-legged creature they could
beg, borrow or steal, the wilder the better, they would
gallop all round the Island demanding largesse from
every house or cottage they passed. They begged, or
rather demanded, for the Island charities, and none
either wished or dared to refuse them, for the splendour
and terror of their passing was a grand, almost elemental
thing, sweeping all before it like one of the great
autumn storms from the sea. . . . The steady approach
of galloping horses in the dark, gunshots and men
shouting, clattering hoofs on the cobbles and hard fists
battering on the door. Then a man's voice shouting:
"Open, M'sieur! Open, M'dame! *Des sous! Des
sous!*" The opening of the door and the sight of
plunging horses, blazing torches and white teeth grinning in blackened faces. Then shouts and laughter and
the chink of coins passing from hand to hand, and the
light flashing and winking upon gay ribbons and the
bright tankards of ale handed up to refresh the thirsty.
Then a few shouted farewells, a few more gunshots,
and galloping hoofs dying away in the darkness. Then
silence again, and the far-off murmur of the sea. . . .
Who shall describe the excitement and thrilling beauty
of the Foresters' Ride?

Every child on the Island possessed of any guts at all
had one overwhelming wish as the Fifth of November
drew near; to take part in the Foresters' Ride. And
every parent on the Island had one great preoccupation

in these autumn days; to take great care that the child did no such thing. For the Foresters were gay before they started on their ride, but at the end of it, after a drink at every house, they were very happy indeed, and casualties were not infrequent. The Foresters on the Fifth of November, declared the Island parents, were not fit company for nicely-brought-up children.

"But we're not nicely-brought-up," said Colin du Frocq to his parents at breakfast on the first of November. "Everyone says we aren't."

"Who says you aren't?" demanded his beautiful mother, Rachell, with dark eyes flashing.

"Everyone," said Colin evasively. "Marmalade, please."

"You *are* nicely-brought-up," declared Rachell angrily. "*Very* nicely-brought-up. You tell the truth. You're brave. If you have more freedom than most children that's because your Father and I think that freedom is good for you."

"Freedom!" snorted Michelle, the eldest of the four girls and one son who were the exhausting quiverful of André du Frocq and his wife. "Do you call it giving us our freedom not to let us join the Foresters' Ride? Slaves in the galleys had more freedom than we have!"

"Upon what," asked André, appearing from behind the newspaper that he always erected in front of himself during family rows, "would you ride in the Foresters' Ride?"

His simmering offspring quieted down, for this

question was something of a poser. André, being a poet-farmer, was not a very successful farmer, and the only animals on the farm of Bon Repos capable of being ridden upon were an ancient horse called Lupin and an even more ancient donkey of the name of Albert. Though five children might conceivably have been crowded upon their two backs it was not conceivable that movement could have been expected under the circumstances.

"Horses would be lent us if we asked for them," said Peronelle airily. She was a lovely child, golden-haired and fairy-like. So enchanting was she in her early 'teens that she had already developed the beautiful woman's certainty that what she wants will be forthcoming.

Her older sister Michelle, dark-haired, clever and plain, had no such expectation. "Who by?" she asked gloomily.

"The new young Seigneur," said Peronelle in her brave clear voice.

"And I said my children were truthful," said Rachell mournfully.

Peronelle flushed and bit her lip. "Sorry," she said. She had lied, and she knew it. The old Lord of the Manor, a kindly and generous old Islander, would have given her anything she asked for, but the nephew from England who had inherited his property was not like that. He had only been on the Island a mere six weeks, and they had not seen him yet, but already they knew the unpleasant sort of young man that he was. People had told them, and they knew, too, because of the way he was behaving over M'sieur Bougourd's wind-mill. Pierre Bougourd, their nearest neighbour, was the best miller and one of the best, most honest and most generous men on the Island, and his glorious wind-mill had come down from father to son for generations. Yet some years ago he had got into trouble, as generous and honest men not infrequently do, and the old Seigneur had had to lend him money to save his mill; money that the old man had said should be paid back entirely at M'sieur Bougourd's convenience. But the new Seigneur was not Island-born; he did not under-stand the leisurely Island methods of conducting financial affairs, nor the comradeship that made the Islanders all one family; to him business was business and debts must be paid. He demanded his pound of flesh. M'sieur Bougourd was being forced to sell his mill.

"Stuck-up, disobliging beast!" said Peronelle, refer-ring to the young Seigneur. "Shylock! Trampler upon the Face of the Poor!"

"And he has such glorious horses!" mourned Michelle. "If only he hadn't been a—what you say —we could have borrowed them all off him."

"You could not," said Rachell. "Under no cir-cumstances will you ever be permitted to take part in the Foresters' Ride."

"But, Mother——" began Colin.

"The discussion is now closed," said André, who for so gentle a man was taking an unusually large part in the morning's argument. "Every year you demand that you shall join the Foresters' Ride. Every year your Mother and I tell you that we shall never give you permission to do so. Every year your Mother's and my digestions are ruined by the scene you make at breakfast. There's been enough of it. I am going round the farm and if anyone wants me I shall not be found." And he went out of the room, closing the door with a vehemence unusual with him.

"Poor Father!" sighed Rachell. "Now you've upset him for the day. It's hard for a poet to have five children."

"It's hard for five children to have a poet for a father," said Colin, who though the youngest but one always had plenty to say for himself. "If Father wasn't a poet he might be a rich man, and then we should have stables full of horses like the young Seigneur."

"But you wouldn't ride in the Foresters' Ride," said his Mother, and she too left the room.

"Oh, wouldn't I!" said Colin naughtily to the closing door.

"You dare speak like that to Mother!" said Peronelle, and picking him up (fairy-like though she might be to look at her sinews were of iron) she pitched him out of the window into a fuchsia bush.

This seemed to clear the air, somehow, and they all felt better.

"It's Saturday, and no lessons," said Jacqueline, the third girl, a pretty dark-haired child, less strong-minded than the others, who took no part in rows but always arrived very pat with a soothing remark when one was over.

"So it is," said Peronelle. "Let's go to the mill."

"Me too!" shouted little Colette. She was a fat creature with golden curls, a fondness for food and that loving disposition that so often goes with rotundity. It was her constant preoccupation not to be left out of anything, for short in the leg as she was, and short in the wind owing to her bulk, she sometimes found it very difficult to keep up. Without a lot of shouting on her part she was apt to be left behind.

"Of course, ducky," said Peronelle, who loved her. "Put on your coat and your gaiters. Quick! Quick!"

Ten minutes later they were marching in military fashion down the lane to the mill, Colin leading the van and Colette trundling along in the rear, gasping and panting, with her gaiters flopping round her ankles.

"Halt!" yelled Peronelle, stopping the detachment. "The commissariat's unbuttoned."

In the children's expeditions Colette was always referred to as the commissariat, for she could always be relied upon to have her pockets stuffed full of things to eat; nuts, apples, bits of sugar, shell-fish even; everything was grist that came to her mill. Her greed was distressing in one so young but was mitigated by her unselfishness in sharing her supplies with others. As she sat on Peronelle's lap beside the lane, having her gaiters buttoned, her fat hand, grasping a headless shrimp by the tail, was held generously out towards Michelle.

"Greedy little cabbage, you!" said Michelle. "Eat it yourself."

Colette, sucking ecstatically, did so, and the march towards the windmill was continued.

IT WAS THE CROWNING GLORY OF A ROUND GREEN HILL

Modern children have many more elaborate amusements than their parents had, but they don't have windmills. It is to be deplored. The du Frocqs, could they have known that in the years to come children would not have windmills, would have been ready to weep for pity. To them the Island windmills were among the greatest of its joys; especially the glorious windmill of M'sieur Bougourd.

It was close to Bon Repos and it was the crowning glory of a round green hill that commanded glorious views of the cliffs and the sea, the pasture lands and harvest fields and grey granite homesteads of the Island. To run up the steep green slope towards it on a day of sun and wind such as was this autumn day, and then to stand with heads tilted back and see its splendid stature reared up against the white-flecked blue sky, with whirring clashing sails revolving so mightily in the sunshine, was to know the very height of delight. There was nothing to compare with that windmill, thought the children; except, of course, the ecstasy of participation in the Foresters' Ride.

They ran up the wooden steps and knocked imperiously upon the door of the mill. It was opened immediately by the obliging M'sieur Bougourd and they tumbled ecstatically in. *"Bonjour, M'sieur!"* they cried. *"Bonjour! Bonjour!"*

"Bonjour, mes enfants!" responded M'sieur Bougourd and his kindly rather careworn face, framed in a fringe of white-dusted whisker, lightened at the sight of them, while his bent shoulders straightened a little. Pierre Bougourd was devoted to children; otherwise

he would not have tolerated the constant raids of the five du Frocqs with such smiling kindliness. The fact was that he was too good-hearted, too ready to help lame dogs over stiles, too willing to have his time wasted by all and sundry. It was his goodness that had been his undoing.

The children thought him a fairy-tale man, the perfect inhabitant for his enchanting mill. They gave squeals of delight as they found themselves once more within its lovely dusty ground-floor room and saw the sun rays, full of dancing dust motes, slanting down through the little square windows and lighting the piled grain stacked round the walls to shimmering gold. "Fairy gold," they called it, and sometimes when M'sieur Bougourd's back was turned they would pick it up in handfuls and let it run through their fingers, remembering the poor old peasant in the Island fairy story who had set a dish of cream for the fairies at sunset beside a pile of grain, and had come down in the morning to find the grain turned into golden pieces. He had been a generous poor man who even in the bitterest poverty had never neglected to give the fairies their cream, and they had not let him go unrewarded.

Colette, even though M'sieur Bougourd was looking, did this now. "Gold!" she crooned, as she let it slip through her fingers. "Fairy gold!"

"*Mon Dieu!*" ejaculated M'sieur Bougourd with sudden bitter vehemence. "Gold! I wish to God it were!"

The children gazed at him in astonishment, for bitterness was unusual with M'sieur Bougourd, but

even as they gazed the black look passed from his face
and he was his usual smiling self again. "Anyone
going up on the sacks?" he asked.

"Yes!" they yelled.

"Meet you at the top," he said, and turned to climb
the upright ladder that passed through each successive
floor of the mill until it reached the little room at the
top where the grain was ground into flour by the action
of the great whirring wings.

The children, however, went up another way. Each
floor of the mill had in its centre a trapdoor, made to
open easily upwards upon slight pressure from below.
Through these trapdoors the sacks of grain travelled
upwards on a rope to the miller in the little room at the
top, who wound up the rope by means of a hand-
turned wheel. Upon the top of each sack as it went up
there now sat a child, clinging to the rope and opening
each trapdoor as it came to it by the pressure of its
own hard bullet-head. . . . Colette alone did not in-
dulge in this pastime, for her head was not hard or
bullety enough yet. In a couple of years' time it
would be, and meanwhile she stayed where she was,
playing with the grain and whispering softly, "Gold,
fairy gold!" She was not lonely, for one of M'sieur
Bougourd's men, Albert Falla, was with her, fastening
the sacks to the rope, and every now and again the other
children would come panting down the ladder to make
the exciting ascent all over again.

They never tired of it. They would have gone on
with it, had they been permitted, all day and all night
for weeks and months. To Colin and Jacqueline the

172

pleasure lay in the movement, the swaying of the rope, the noise of the whirring wings and the tremor of the whole mill to their rhythm. But to Michelle and Peronelle it meant more than this, it meant the exciting feeling that they were for the moment a part of this grand bit of machinery devised for the creation of the bread of the world. They were thrilled by the romance of the mill, by its power and beauty.

But to-day Peronelle found herself not so full of enjoyment as usual. She was much troubled by that bitter ejaculation of M'sieur Bougourd's. "Gold! I wish to God it were!" As she swayed upwards through one trapdoor after the other she looked through the little windows of the mill at the glorious views of fields and sea and high driving clouds and wondered just how unhappy M'sieur Bougourd was. If she herself cared so much for this wonderful mill how much more must M'sieur Bougourd care for it, in whose family it had been for so many years. Their farm of Bon Repos had been in their family for centuries and she remembered her father's misery when they were once so poor that he had thought they would have to sell it. . . . People like the young Seigneur, inheriting a property they had scarcely ever seen, could not know how one felt about a possession that one had grown up with, that was bone of one's bone and soul of one's soul. . . . Thinking of the young Seigneur she ground her teeth furiously together.

"Beast!" she said. "But I'll get even with him somehow. I'll save M'sieur Bougourd's mill." And she shut her pretty mouth very firmly indeed. Her good friend Pierre Bougourd was not going to suffer this grief. She would see to it. She was capable, she thought, of seeing to anything. Her faith in her own powers was colossal, but justified, for she had such a way with her that even fate gave in to Peronelle sometimes.

It was in this frame of mind that she made her sixth ascent and slid off her sack in the top room. But she did not immediately climb down the ladder again, as the others did, but went to stand beside Pierre Bougourd where he stood turning his great wheel. "M'sieur," she said, "do you believe in those old stories about the fairy gold?"

"Eh?" said M'sieur Bougourd, for it was difficult to hear her above the roar that was going on.

Peronelle repeated her question, and added: "I've been told again and again that if you put cream for the fairies at sunset beside a pile of grain you're sure to find the grain turned to gold in the morning. . . . But you have to have an honest and good heart."

M'sieur Bougourd smiled at her tolerantly.

"You don't believe them?" she insisted.

M'sieur Bougourd, who would sooner have died than shatter the faith of a child, though he was astonished that Peronelle at her age should still believe in those pretty but fabulous tales, compressed his face into becoming gravity and assured her that he did. "But certainly," he said forcibly. "Certainly."

"Then why don't you do it?" she said. "Why don't you do it, M'sieur Bougourd? Don't you want the money?"

M'sieur swung round on her and his kindly face was crimson with rage. "Who says I want money?" he said fiercely. "If you've been listening to gossip I'll thank you to keep your mouth shut!"

Peronelle was not frightened at his wrath. It must be very vexing for a proud man to suspect that the whole Island was pitying him. There is something slightly insulting about pity. She looked into his angry eyes without blinking and said steadily, "If anyone has an honest and good heart it must be you."

M'sieur Bougourd swung away from her again. "It don't pay in this world," he muttered savagely. "The Bible may say it do, but it don't. . . . Here, you young varmints, what are you doing two on one sack? Haven't I told you it must be one at a time or not at all? The rope can't stand the strain, as I've told you fifty times if once."

Jacqueline and Colin had done the forbidden thing and come up together clinging to the same sack. They now fell off it and rolled on to his feet, causing his already greatly strained patience to give way altogether.

"Now you get along home!" he thundered. "Why I have you here, God knows. My arm is nearly out of its socket with winding you up and down on this damn rope all day long. Now you take yourselves off before I take a stick to the lot of you."

Michelle arrived up on another sack to hear this last remark, and immediately marshalled her younger brothers and sisters towards the ladder. The du Frocq children never stayed where they were not wanted. They had their pride.

"If you don't want us of course we will go at once," she said with frigid politeness. "Good morning, M'sieur. Say good morning to M'sieur Bougourd, you others."

"Good morning, M'sieur," said Jacqueline.

"Good morning, M'sieur," said Colin.

"Good morning, M'sieur," said Michelle once again, and the three of them sank from sight with the dignity of three submerging porpoises who feel their morals contaminated by intercourse with the upper air.

Peronelle lingered a moment. "Just try it," she urged. "Try it on the Fifth of November when you shut the mill up for the night. Put a saucer of cream beside the grain at sunset. Please. One of us will come round to see that you really *do* it. Good morning, M'sieur." And she too sank from sight down the ladder, her lovely upturned laughing face, framed in golden hair, seeming to float upon the shadows below like the face of a water nymph upon a dark wave. Left alone M'sieur Bougourd cursed himself for his loss of temper. In the company of children a man may at least find refuge from the torment of his own thoughts.

Out upon the green hillside, going rather disconsolately homewards, Peronelle made haste to soothe the ruffled feelings of the others. "He can't help it," she said. "He's going bankrupt. Don't you remember how snappy Father got when he thought he was?"

The others were very sorry indeed; and Colette, always very full of sensibility, removed the apple she was gnawing from her mouth in order to weep a bit.

"Don't cry, ducky," said Peronelle. "We aren't

176

going to let the poor man go bankrupt. We're going to do something about it."

"What?" asked Colin. "Colette, could I have the core of your apple? I haven't had an apple for days."

"There isn't going to be a core," sobbed Colette, and ate it, pips and all.

"Yes, what?" said Michelle. "I don't see what there is that we can do about it."

"I'm about to have one of my Inspirations," said Peronelle portentously. "I can feel it coming on. I had the first preliminary chinks of light in the mill and the final illumination is not far away." She dropped her voice impressively, as she had once heard a lecturer on the occult do, and waved her hand towards the horizon.

"Don't be a fool!" her brother and sisters adjured her. They nevertheless looked at her with interest and cheered up a good deal. For Peronelle's Inspirations, though they might be devastating, were never dull. If they did not always achieve their object they at least caused a grand upheaval for all concerned.

During dinner it was obvious even to Peronelle's anxious parents that an Inspiration was on the way. They knew the signs, and their hearts failed within them. One of these signs was a rapt and far-away gaze, another was a marked increase in appetite, a third was a burning interest in moral problems.

For Peronelle, before embarking upon any cataclysmic course of action, liked to feel that she had the approval of her conscience. It was as necessary to her happiness that she should feel she was battling for the right as it was necessary that she should do what she wanted to do, and from long practice her mind was wonderfully agile in giving arguments the bias required.

"Father," said Peronelle, "don't you think that very often the end justifies the means?"

"No," said André firmly.

"Well, I do," said Peronelle. "I think that if I saw a poor lame man unable to walk to his work, and I knew of a rich man who had a horse and wasn't lending it to him, I should be perfectly justified in taking the horse to help the lame man."

"That would be stealing," said André. "It is never right to do evil that good may come."

"Then I must let the poor man suffer?" demanded Peronelle indignantly. "I call that downright wicked, Father."

André thrust his hands through his already considerably rumpled hair (a poem had not been going well that morning) and looked despairingly at his wife.

"The thing to do in a case like that, Peronelle," said Rachell with brisk decision, "is not to steal somebody else's horse for the lame man but to give him one of your own."

"But I haven't got one of my own," explained Peronelle. "And who said I was going to steal? I wasn't. I was just going to borrow the horse without permission."

"But why not ask for permission?" asked her father.

"Because I know it would be refused."

"To borrow without permission, and without the certainty that you will be able to return what you have taken, *is* stealing," said André.

"I don't think so," said Peronelle. "When I lent your umbrella the other day to M'dame Ferbrache and told you afterwards what I'd done you said: 'Good girl'."

"In the mere matter of an umbrella——" began André, but his daughter interrupted him.

"You've told me again and again," she said, "that the same laws of good conduct apply to little and big things. Therefore if it was right for me to take your umbrella for M'dame Ferbrache, it will be right for me to take a rich man's horse to help a poor man, and the end does justify the means and I'd like a little more pudding. Mother, I didn't tell you that I am top of my class again, and all the girls think I shall get the form prize for good conduct."

As usual, she had swept her parents along with her own impetus, and they found themselves discussing her school affairs instead of thrashing out the matter of the poor lame man and the horse, and all its possibly alarming implications, an omission they were to regret before many days were over.

"And so you see," said Peronelle to her brother and sisters when their exhausted parents had left them to finish their third helpings of pudding by themselves, "it will be perfectly right for us to steal the Seigneur's horses—temporarily, of course—and ride in the Foresters' Ride even though we've been told not to, because by begging at the houses we shall get enough

money to save M'sieur Bougourd's mill. The end
justifies the means. Mother and Father said so."

"Did they?" said Michelle. "I thought they said
it didn't."

"I brought them round," said Peronelle. "Didn't
you follow the argument?"

Colin let out a whoop of joy and performed cart-
wheels round the table. What cared he for arguments,
moral or otherwise? Four days later they would be
riding in the Foresters' Ride.

It took them the whole of that four days to lay their
plans, for Peronelle, like all good generals, understood
the value of meticulous care in preparation. The
evening of the Fifth found them getting ready with
every detail of their movements and costume planned
down to the last minute and the last pin. It was
difficult to see how anything could go wrong. They
were full of confidence, as they gathered in Michelle's
bedroom, and full of happiness. . . . All except Colette,
who was weeping great fat tears the size of marbles. . . .
For she was not to be allowed to take part in the
Foresters' Ride. It was considered that she was too
little, and too fat. She invariably fell off even when
placed upon Albert the donkey, so what, the others
asked her, did she think she would do if placed upon
one of the Seigneur's fiery horses? "Stay on," she
said, and sobbed afresh; but quietly, because to have
cried with her usual noise and abandon would have
been to endanger the success of the whole adventure. . . .
She was an unselfish child.

"You're to take the cream to the mill, ducky, you're to take it all by yourself," Peronelle reminded her with the intent to comfort.

Colette stuck out her lower lip and kicked the chair she was sitting on very naughtily with her thick outdoor boots. Was taking cream to the mill any consolation for having a white face when all the others had black ones? None at all.

She gazed at them, distracted with envy. They had blacked their hands and faces with burnt cork and donned coloured jerseys above their riding breeches, whose pockets were filled with apples and sugar for the Seigneur's horses. They had hung all the bead necklaces they could find round their necks and stuck peacocks' feathers into ribbons tied round their heads. The three girls had large brass curtain rings tied on to their ears for earrings and Colin had his toy pistol stuck in his belt. They looked magnificent; especially Peronelle, whose curly fair hair was in striking contrast to her blackened face and scarlet jersey.

Skilfully, for they had done it so often before, they descended from Michelle's bedroom window on to the top of the water-butt, and from there to the vegetable-marrow bed. Then, faintly jingling, they stole through the shadows of the kitchen garden and out into the lane.

It was the hour of sunset. The Foresters' Ride started at dark from the Inn of M'sieur le Tissier at Mahy Bay, but the windmill was on their way to the Seigneur's stables and they were anxious to see little Colette safely through her bit of adventure before they left her. They hid in a little copse at the bottom of the green hill where the windmill stood and rehearsed her carefully in her part.

Buttoned up warmly in her scarlet reefer coat, with a little red dahlia stuck in her buttonhole to comfort her, the tears not yet dry on her face, and her hair a halo of gold round her head in the sunset light, she stood up before them with a saucer in one hand and a jug of cream stolen from the larder in the other, and told them what she had to do.

"I'm to knock at the door," she whispered breathlessly, "and M'sieur Bougourd will be inside shuttin' up for the night. I'm to give him the cream an' the saucer an' tell him to pour it out an' put it beside the grain for the fairies, so that in the mornin' the grain shall be gold. Then when we're outside again, an' M'sieur Bougourd has locked the mill, I'm to see where he puts the key an' come back an' tell you."

The whispering little voice ceased abruptly and she sobbed. Then putting down the jug of cream she felt in the pocket of her reefer coat and produced a peppermint bull's-eye and the rear portion of what had once been a sugar mouse. With these thrust one into each cheek for comfort she started on her journey up the hill.

The others watched her plodding little figure with compunction. It is hard to be so little that you can't do really exciting things. It is hard to be the youngest and have to play the part of Ganymede to the gods upon Olympus. They had all, of course, had to take their turn at being Ganymede, but Colette's turn was lasting longer than anyone else's had, so slow was

Mother in producing another baby to relieve her. It really was hardly fair. Mother must be spoken to about it.

Then they forgot their compunction in the enchantment of the moment. It was a dry, warm November, and such a wonderfully still evening that they could hear the far-away murmur of the sea and the clop-clop of a horse's hoofs in the distant lane. The windmill, with its great wings quite still, stood up black and strong against a western sky of sheeted gold, its great purple shadow stretching out down the green hill to envelop the little scarlet-coated figure of Colette. They watched her climb the steps to the mill and hammer on the closed door with both her little clenched fists. They saw the door open, a chink of light shining out through it, and Colette step inside. Then the door shut again and they had to imagine the scene within.

It wasn't difficult, for they knew both M'sieur Bougourd and Colette. He would stoop and thrust a forefinger through one of her round sausage curls, just as he always did, and then he would laugh at her request that he should pour out the cream for the fairies. But he would not refuse it. Not for the world would he disappoint Colette. They could picture him solemnly setting the saucer beside the pile of grain, and solemnly filling it from the little jug that Colette had brought him.

Then the door opened again and the two came out, and M'sieur Bougourd turned to lock the door behind him. From where they were hiding the children could not see what he did with the key but they could see that Colette, according to instructions, was watching very carefully.

But now came the first deviation from plan, for instead of going off down the other side of the hill to his home, as they had expected him to do, M'sieur Bougourd came down their side of the hill with Colette. The tiresome man evidently thought it his duty to see her safely home. Now what were they to do? A long-drawn sigh of despair burst from four pairs of lips.

But they had reckoned without Colette. That little lady, though young, was wily. Halfway down the hill she stopped and held up her fat arms to M'sieur Bougourd, asking to be taken pick-a-back. Her reason for this was clear when she came level with the little copse where her brother and sisters were hiding. "Gee-up, Dobbin!" she cried loudly to M'sieur Bougourd, and bounced solidly upon the poor man's back, digging her heels into him as she would have done into the leathery sides of Albert the donkey, and causing the poor man such pain that he was conscious of no extra physical sensation when leaning to one side she plunged a hand into his pocket, took out a key and tossed it into the copse.

"Good little pet!" chuckled Peronelle when Colette and M'sieur Bougourd were out of sight and hearing. "Wasn't she clever?"

"We've trained her well," said Michelle.

"I hope she won't give us away when Father and Mother ask where we are," said Jacqueline anxiously.

"Not she," said Colin darkly. "She knows I'd skin her alive if she did."

It's hard being the youngest.

Now came the most hazardous part of the whole adventure. Crouched in the ditch outside the gate that led into the Seigneur's stable yard the four listened anxiously. They did not speak for each child was afraid that a slight quavering of the voice might betray an unseen nervousness that each would rather have died than admit. There was not a sound and they stole out.

Fortune favours the brave. When they crept into the yard there was not a soul to be seen, and the door to the loose-boxes was not fastened. They had chosen their moment well, for the stablemen had gone indoors for the high tea of lobster and blackberry jam which is a feature of Island life about the hour of sunset, and the new young Seigneur, who was so stuck-up and disobliging, was no doubt indoors too, being disobliging in his own luxurious quarters.

Through the unlatched half-door they surveyed the contents of the loose-boxes, and the contents of the loose-boxes, rolling the whites of their eyes and chewing their tea, surveyed them.

Three fine riding horses, one young and fiery, jet-black with a white star on his forehead, another not so young, chestnut brown and gentle-eyed, and a third quite white and beautiful as a hawthorn tree in the spring; these were doubtless ridden by the Seigneur himself, or driven in his high dashing dogcart. Then there was a stout dappled cob who they knew trundled the trap into the town when the housekeeper did her shopping, and a mouse-coloured pony who perhaps pulled the mowing machine. . . . There was one mount each and one to spare.

"Bags I the black one with the white star," panted Peronelle. "I've always wanted to ride a black horse!"

"You'll do no such thing," said Michelle firmly. "By the look of him he'd kill you. He'd kill any of us. We'll leave him behind. After all, I think Father's and Mother's feelings do deserve some consideration. They've not been bad parents on the whole."

Peronelle reluctantly gave in. She was fond of her parents.

They went to the harness-room and picked out the saddles and bridles they wanted. There was still a lot of light in the sky, though one star shone over the stable yard. Then quickly and skilfully they set about the harnessing of the chestnut horse, the white horse, the dappled cob and the mousy pony.

It might have been supposed that these creatures would have protested. But they didn't. There is a secret communion between animals and children who love them that a grown-up cannot quite attain to, and a horse, in a greater degree than any animal except perhaps an elephant, can feel the vibrations that come from a human mind. And the vibrations in this case were those of affection, trust, utter fearlessness, and delight in the thought of a great adventure. The horses responded at once; especially after the mastication of an apple and four lumps of sugar each. Without a single scuffle of protestation they suffered themselves to be harnessed, led out of their stables, mounted, and ridden out into the darkening lane. . . . The only person who behaved other than excellently was the black horse with the white star on his forehead and he, left all alone, whinnied so furiously, so long and so loud, that the children looked at each other in dismay.

"He's telling the Seigneur!" ejaculated Michelle.

"It's all right," said Peronelle. "We're well away."

The Foresters met on the little patch of green before Le Tissier's Inn, built on the cliffs above rocky Mahy Bay. When the children arrived they were already gathering and the scene was exciting beyond their wildest expectations. From the old grey granite inn, with its deep-set windows and wide-flung doorway, the light streamed out to illumine the jostling crowd of restless, excited horses and laughing men with white teeth flashing in their blackened faces. They were most of them as gaily dressed as the children and the whole scene was a brilliant kaleidoscope of colour gathered together like a bright pool in the hollow of the darkening night. Far down below them the waves broke on the rocks of Mahy Bay. Their thunder was an exciting accompaniment to the whole gay mad scene.

Anyone who liked might join the Foresters' Ride. No questions were ever asked. A few quizzical glances were flung at the children, and there were laughing comments at the sight of Peronelle's black face in its aureole of golden hair, but they and their mounts were absorbed into the pool of light with an instant friendliness that warmed their hearts. There is no friendliness like the friendliness of thieves, no bond so strong as common banditry.

The torches were lit, a gun was fired, and with a shout they were off, wheeling up the tree-shadowed lane two abreast, glittering and triumphant. At the top of the hill, at the cross-roads out in the open, they paused, waiting for stragglers, and perhaps awed in spite of themselves by the star-spangled stretch of the night sky over their heads. In the pause the sound of galloping hoofs came very clearly.

"Wait!" called the burly young farmer who seemed the leader of this expedition. "Let him catch up."

The late-comer was approaching from the direction from which the children had come. So exciting was the sound of his galloping hoofs in the darkness that all heads were turned eagerly in his direction as he breasted the hill and joined them. They were not disappointed. With superb horsemanship, and as though of right, he wheeled his horse in beside the leader, raised his whip in salute, and swept the whole cavalcade forward as though by his own impetus. . . . He seemed a king among men.

But who was he? No one seemed to know, and the question was eagerly debated by those who rode near the children. He rode as the Islanders, more at home in a boat than on horseback, had never seen a man ride before, as though he and his fine black horse were one creature. "Like a centaur," whispered Peronelle to Colin. "See how straight his back is." Colin nodded, speechless with admiration, hot with sudden, flaming hero-worship, pushing the chestnut horse that he rode a little nearer to his god. Peronelle on the white horse followed him. Michelle on the dappled cob stayed with Jacqueline, who was not such an expert rider as the others and so had been given the quiet mousy pony.

Close behind the unknown rider Peronelle and Colin could take in the details of his appearance. He wore a superbly cut black riding coat and black top-boots so well polished that they shone like glass, and a hard black hat stuck at a rakish angle. He had not blacked his face but when he turned his head they could see that he wore a little black carnival mask through which his eyes shone with a rather alarming glitter. Below it his chin and jaw showed white and clearly-cut, hard and resolute. The only touch of colour was a scarlet hand-kerchief stuck jauntily in his pocket. So black and white was he, so sinister with that touch of scarlet, that he might have been Mephistopheles out for the evening.

They had reached the first farm and clattered into its courtyard with their yells of "*Des doubles, M'sieur et M'dame! Des sous!*" The leader jumped from his horse and hammered on the door and out came the farmer and his wife, laughing but slightly alarmed, to hand out mugs of ale and all the small change they could lay their hands on. The children, as they had promised each other they would do, pushed through the good-natured Foresters and getting to the front of the crowd got a generous share of the loot; especially golden-haired Peronelle on her white horse.

"It's for a good purpose," she cried to those about her. "It's for charity. It's to help the poor."

"*Mais oui*," cried the Foresters. "All for charity. *Dieu vous garde, M'sieur. Dieu vous garde, M'dame.*" And wiping their mouths on the backs of their hands they handed back the mugs and gave the signal to pass on for the next raid.

Pressing forward as they had the children had made themselves conspicuous. They now found themselves trotting on all together in a little group with the stranger in their midst. They had not meant to absorb him in this way; they rather thought it was he who had inserted himself among them, and he who had seen to it that Peronelle was on his right, Colin on his left and the other two on ahead.

"I admire your mounts," he said in a cold, clear, crisp voice. "A white horse, a chestnut horse, a dappled cob and mousy pony. They make a delightful quartette."

"I admire yours," responded Peronelle politely, though for some unaccountable reason her heart was beating so fast that she found it quite difficult to speak. "I have always longed to ride a black horse."

"His back legs are not entirely trustworthy," said the stranger. "That's why I've sent the other two little kids on ahead."

His remark stung Peronelle. "My eldest sister and I are in our 'teens," she said loftily.

The stranger bowed to her.

"And I'm eleven," said Colin. But he was not aggrieved, he was merely wanting to tell his god about himself. "I play rugger," he added.

"And I don't doubt you play it jolly well," said the god kindly. "You certainly sit a borrowed mount several sizes too large for you with uncommon skill."

Peronelle looked up sharply, and just at that moment the black horse turned its head and whinnied softly and companionably to the white horse. It had a white star on its forehead, and at sight of it Peronelle knew why her heart was beating. Colin, she could see, chatting about this and that, remained in happy ignorance as to the identity of his god. The other two, on ahead, could not see the white star, and slow in the uptake as they were would probably have guessed nothing if they had. While Peronelle was wondering what to do they arrived at the next farm and the rider on the black horse slipped into the background while the looting went forward. When it was over, however, he rejoined the children and hoped they had done well.

"Very well, thank you," said Peronelle.

"This systematic plunder is to benefit the hospital and the Governor's Christmas Fund, so I understand?"

"Most of them are collecting for the charities you mention," said Peronelle with dignity. "My brother and sisters and I are collecting for a private charity."

"Ah," said the stranger. "I thought there was some deep and Machiavellian purpose at work here."

The next farm they came to was Bon Repos and letting the others clatter on ahead into the courtyard the children stayed outside in the lane. The stranger stayed with them.

"Your parents live here?" he asked affably.

Peronelle scowled at him. "How do you know?" she demanded.

"This sudden shyness. This desire not to be seen at this particular house. This adventure is no doubt taking place without parental permission?"

Peronelle hated him. The cold yet somehow silky voice, the shining polish of his appearance, the sarcasm, it was all quite detestable. Yet she could not help admiring the way he sat his horse and the way he kept his temper. . . . He must be longing to get his whip about their ears.

After they left the next few farms the Foresters' Ride began to gather impetus. Excitement, inflamed by liquid refreshment, was mounting. There were catcalls, shouts and laughter. Rattles were brandished, whistles shrilled and guns went off. The torches streamed in the wind and the sound of the cantering hoofs was like thunder on the road. It was thrilling, but it was also a little terrifying. It was more terrifying than the children had known it would be and they were actually glad to have the stranger with them. His quick staccato injunctions to them to grip with their knees, to hold their horses' heads up and keep their wits about them, kept them time and again from disaster. At one inn, at a cross-roads not far from M'sieur Bougourd's windmill, where the tumult outside was almost matched by the tumult inside, he made the children turn back with him into a quiet meadow beside the road, where a tinkling stream emptied itself into a round still pond where the stars were reflected like silver nails studding an ebony shield.

"Too much row going on there for little kids," he said. "And the horses need a drink."

They were all glad to rest. The children let the reins go slack with sighs of relief and the horses' soft noses nuzzled the star-spangled water. The night wind rustled in the trees and the sound of the riot in the inn yard came to them only very distantly.

"About this private charity," said the stranger. "How's it getting on? The hour is late, you know, and the horses are dead-beat. I should say it was time we made tracks for home."

"We've not nearly enough money yet," said Colin. "And if you keep holding us back whenever we get anywhere we never shall have," he added in an aggrieved tone.

"How much are you hoping to collect?" asked the stranger, "and what's it for? A horse apiece?"

Peronelle came to a sudden decision. She would make a clean breast of it. "It's not for ourselves we're collecting," she said. "It's to save M'sieur Bougourd's windmill."

"To save M'sieur Bougourd's windmill?" ejaculated the stranger.

"I'll tell you," said Peronelle. "M'sieur is a very good, honest, generous man, but he's too generous, too honest, and he never seems able to make much money. He got into debt and had to borrow money off his landlord the old Seigneur. The old Seigneur was very glad to lend it to him, for he was fond of M'sieur Bougourd and did not want him to have to sell his mill, for the Bougourds have owned that mill for generations. The old Seigneur knew what a good thing it is to have families working on the land who have been there for years and years. He liked to have men like that on his estate. He would have let M'sieur Bougourd pay him back very gradually and would never have pressed him for the money. The old Seigneur was a very kind man. He was like a father to his people. It was a dreadful thing for us all when he died."

She paused and the wind sighed again in the trees.

"The old Seigneur died," she went on, "and now there is a new Seigneur, his nephew. He has come from England and he doesn't understand Island ways very well yet. He doesn't know how patient we always are with each other, and how being on an Island one has to be very kindly and friendly because the sea all round us makes us, so to speak, all one family. He says that M'sieur Bougourd must pay his debts at once, and poor M'sieur Bougourd is afraid he will have to sell the windmill that belonged to his father, and his grand-father, and his great-grandfather before that."

"Beast!" said Colin, referring to the new Seigneur.

"So the charitable collection is to save M'sieur Bougourd's windmill," repeated the stranger.

"Yes," said Peronelle, and told him about poor little Colette, too young to share this adventure, and the dish of cream, and the fairy story of the grain that was turned to gold.

"We will put this money beside the grain to-night," she said, "and when he finds it in the morning he won't know who put it there."

"Won't he?" said the stranger. "Perhaps not; he is a singularly obtuse man. So you think that this little collection of doubles and sous is going to be enough to save the mill, do you?"

"Not at this rate," growled Colin; the Foresters' Ride was getting noisily under way again and his god was making no move to join it.

"And not at any rate," said the stranger. "You'd never make enough in one night of highway robbery to save that mill."

He took a pencil and a pad of paper from his pocket and holding it on his knee, began writing busily by the light of the moon.

"Be quick! Oh, be quick!" begged Michelle. "The Foresters are off again!"

"We're not off with them," said the stranger. "The Foresters' Ride, at this stage, is no place for well-brought-up children and horses. We're off to M'sieur Bougourd's mill. You've got the key safely?"

"What's the use?" groaned Colin, discouraged and irritable with fatigue. "We've not enough money, and never would have, you say."

"This," said the stranger, folding the piece of paper upon which he had been writing, "will mean as much to M'sieur Bougourd as several sacks of gold."

"What is it?" demanded Michelle, wide-eyed.

"Just a letter," said the stranger, and gathering up his reins he wheeled his horse through the gate of the meadow and up the lane that led to the mill. The children followed him, bewildered and blundering with fatigue. . . . All except Peronelle, who was starry-eyed and rode as lightly as a fairy's child.

.   .   .   .   .

M'sieur Bougourd's windmill was an enchanting place at any time, but by silver moonlight it was fairy-land itself. Its great still arms were silver against the sky and the shadow of it stretched down the hill to gather them in. They left their mounts, silver horses upon a field argent, and went in. Moonlight streamed through the windows, silvering the cobwebs in dark corners and showing the saucer of cream upon the floor beside a heap of golden grain. A little red autumn dahlia, presumably dropped out of Colette's buttonhole, lay there too. There was no sound in the stillness except the scurrying flight of a mouse, and there was something strangely peaceful and touching about the scene. The stranger, seeing the inside of a windmill for the first time, took off his hat, as though he indeed felt himself standing upon fairy ground. Then he laid his letter on the floor beside the saucer of cream, with Colette's dahlia on top of it to keep it in place, and silently led the way out. . . . He would not let them put the money they had collected with it; better, he said, to give it to the Governor's Christmas Fund. . . . Silently he locked the door, slipping the key underneath it, and silently they all mounted the silver horses and rode off down the field argent.

None of them spoke until they were at the bottom of the hill, when the stranger said: "I suggest that I see you safely home and then return these weary beasts whence they came."

"Thank you," said Peronelle. "Thank you for everything. I did call you Shylock, and a Trampler upon the Face of the Poor, but I'm sorry now." And they rode on, the others much mystified but far too tired to reason anything out.

At the entrance to the Bon Repos courtyard they dismounted and lifted weary faces to bid their friend good-bye. He took off his hat and bowed to them. "My condolences to Mademoiselle Colette and my compliments to Madame your mother," he said. "I hope I may be allowed to call upon her very shortly. It will be a pleasure to renew acquaintance with you. Meanwhile I am grateful for an excellent lesson on the duties of an Island Seigneur. I needed teaching. Good night."

He was off on his tired black horse, followed by the white horse, the chestnut horse, the dappled cob and the mousy pony. Their hoofs went clip-clop, clip-clop down the quiet lane and the six of them were lost in the moonlight. The children turned on lagging feet to face irate parents.

"Who on earth was he?" asked Jacqueline.

"Mephistopheles," said Michelle.

"A centaur," said Colin.

"Idiots! Duffers! Owls!" said Peronelle. "He was the young Seigneur."

They gaped at her.

"The young Seigneur," she repeated. "We misjudged him. He's charming, and he has a grand seat on a horse, and Mother will like him."

"Why?" asked Colin.

"He said we were well-brought-up."

Chapter Eight

MIDNIGHT IN THE STABLE

IT was the snow that made that Christmas such an extra special one. They did not often see snow in the Channel Islands, and never before in the children's memory had it come at Christmas. It began two days before Christmas Day, soft white flakes drifting down out of an iron-grey sky, and by Christmas Eve, when the sky cleared and the sun appeared again, it had spread over their familiar home a beauty so new and so exciting that they could scarcely contain themselves.

The old rose-red roof of the weather-worn farmhouse where they lived was flecked with white, as though some one had scattered an armful of white flowers over it, and on each of the windows the frost had traced delicate outlines of ferns and grasses. The garden and court-yard were hidden beneath a spread coverlet of gleaming white, and under the bright sunshine and the deep blue sky each frosted twig on bush or tree shone like silver wire. The farm's name of Bon Repos suited it in this weather. A great reposeful silence gripped the world; there was nothing to be heard but the faint mrmuur of the sea beyond their garden and the chirping of the robins about their door.

The children fed these robins to bursting point, and it

was the sight of the little red-breasts bobbing about on the snow like lighted lanterns, and chirping so cheerfully in the intervals of refreshing themselves, that gave Colin du Frocq his bright idea. "Let *us* have lanterns, girls," he said to his four sisters, "and go out carol singing."

"Carol singing in the snow on Christmas Eve!" cried golden-haired Peronelle, jigging for joy. "Good idea, Colin!"

"Would it interfere with hanging up our stockings?" asked Jacqueline anxiously.

"No," said Colin. "We'd hang them up, go to bed, say good night to the parents and then get up again."

"But would the parents approve?" asked Michelle, the bespectacled eldest, a little primly.

"Can't say," said Colin. "Better not ask them. We've never been told *not* to go carol singing."

But little Colette, the baby of the family and the only one who still believed in Father Christmas, waxed a little tearful. "If he comes and finds us gone," she wailed, "he won't put anything in our stockings."

"Leave it to me, darling," consoled Peronelle. "*I'll* see to it. We'll write a note to Father Christmas. 'Dear Sir, The du Frocqs are out but will be returning shortly. Please leave the customary seasonable gifts. Yours truly, the du Frocqs.'"

It was after the midday dinner and the five of them stood outside the front door in the old cobbled courtyard, rosy-cheeked and radiant and apparently entirely oblivious of the cold that had fallen like a blight upon shivering grown-ups. Michelle and Peronelle, who were both in their teens, had gone so far as to put on thin coats over their dark blue serge skirts and red jerseys, and Jacqueline's pretty face was framed in the green knitted scarf she had thrown over her dark curls as an opening flower is framed in its calyx, but the wicked bright-eyed Colin had burdened himself with no outdoor garments, and fat little Colette, wrapped so snugly in layer upon layer of soft dimpled flesh, quantities of flannel petticoats and vests, with a sky-blue woollen frock smocked in scarlet over all, would by the addition of an overcoat have been rendered too hot to move. They were all five so young that newly-lit life tingled to the end of every finger-tip and sprang and sparkled in hair and eyes; there was as yet no slackening of its flame or fading of its warmth.

"We'll spend the afternoon in the stable," said Colin. "No one hears us in the stable. We'll practise the carols there and make ourselves lanterns out of the mangel-wurzels. . . . Listen, is that the bus?"

"The bus!" yelled Colette in triumph, and trundled hastily across the courtyard to the doorway leading into the lane, the others following helter-skelter.

At that time, the end of the nineteenth century, a few farms and a fishing hamlet were the only human habitations in the wild and beautiful part of the Island where they lived, and their one link with the town of St. Pierre, a few miles away, was the daily horse bus. Its arrival was at all times an excitement, for it brought them their visitors, groceries, newspapers and shell-fish. Absolutely anything might arrive off that bus, anything from a visiting uncle to a crab for dinner, and at Christmas time, when presents from admiring friends were to be expected, the arrival of the bus became not only an interesting event but a world-shaking cataclysm.

The children, cantering like young ponies, reached the bus stopping-place, where four lanes met just beyond their farmhouse, just as Jean the bus driver reined in his two ancient horses and brought the clattering old vehicle to a standstill.

"Anything for us?" they yelled to Jean, their eyes going to the box beside him where the parcels were piled.

"Not to-day, praise be," said Jean, winking one eye at them. "I've had my bus so weighed down with parcels for you youngsters this last week that the springs is broke. To-day, I thank *le bon Dieu*, I've travelled light."

"Oh!" chorused the children sadly. "Beast!" they continued good-humouredly. "Merry Christmas!"

"Merry Christmas!" echoed Jean, and then, turning his head over his shoulder. "This is where you get out, Mamselle."

The children turned their attention from the parcels outside the bus to the passengers inside. They knew most of them; a couple of old fisher-wives from the hamlet of Breton Bay, the woman from the Post Office and the travelling tinker; but they did not know the girl whom Jean addressed as Mamselle.

Yet, as they stood beside the bus watching her get out, they wished they did know her, for in spite of the clothes that she wore, the clothes of a beggar-maid, she was attractive. Her dark eyes had the softness of black pansies in her white heart-shaped face, and the hair that escaped from under the shawl that she wore over her head clung round her forehead in enchanting brown curls. Not even her broken black button boots, her frayed black skirt, her rusty shawl and the disreputable carpet bag she carried could hide her slender beauty. She was like a flower, a snowdrop or a Christmas rose or a white camelia, and when she stumbled a little in getting out of the bus, for she had the carpet bag in one hand and was holding something large and heavy in the folds of her shawl with the other, the children rushed to help her as though she had been the Queen.

"*Merci, mes enfants*," she said laughing. "If you had not helped me I might have bumped my baby."

"Have you a baby?" they chorused in joy. "A baby? Quick! Let's see!" And they in their fresh young beauty closed in upon hers like the petals of a flower about the golden heart. The bus turned and rolled away again, the other passengers took their ways home with backward glances of amusement, but the six worshipping the baby were too absorbed to notice.

And certainly it was an enchanting baby, as enchanting as its mother. It was round and fat, and deliciously creased and dimpled. Its eyes were dark, and solemn with the deep solemnity of the very new, but young as it was it had already learnt to be amused, for it laughed when Colette was lifted up to kiss it and its kicking feet and brandished fists were busy establishing contact with a world that seemed good to it. It had no hair at all upon its head, but this, somehow, seemed to the children an added attraction. . . . A nice baby.

"A boy?" asked Peronelle, holding out a slim fore-finger to be gripped by engaging dimpled fingers with nails so tiny that they made her heart miss a beat.

"Of course," said the girl in the slightly superior tone adopted by the mothers of sons.

"Isn't he good!" whispered Jacqueline, clasping a booted foot.

"He never cried the whole way over," triumphed his mother.

"Over?" asked Michelle. "Where have you come from?"

"From France, Mamselle," said the girl. "I have just landed."

"But where are you going?" demanded Colin. "Who are you?"

The girl's soft face suddenly hardened. "That is my affair, little M'sieur," she said. "And now I must ask you to let me go on my way."

"We'll take you," said Colin gallantly. "I'll carry your bag."

"No," said the girl firmly. "Do you live here? In this farmhouse? Your mother would not like you to be out in this bitter cold with so little on to keep you warm. I will watch you run home."

At the door into the courtyard they turned round to wave and saw her still standing at the place where the four lanes met. "Good-bye," they shouted. "Merry Christmas!"

"Merry Christmas!" she called back, and nodded and

smiled as they turned in and were hidden from her sight.

"She was very anxious to get rid of us, wasn't she?" said Jacqueline, aggrieved.

"I don't think she wanted us to see which way she was going," said Peronelle, a little puzzled.

"Clever!" mocked Colin. "She was just being grown-up and officious. She hasn't been grown-up for very long, either, and those new grown-ups are always the worst."

Further argument was quenched by an explosion of tears from Colette that for its suddenness, noise and wetting quality was like the bursting of a cistern.

"I want a baby!" she wailed. "I want a baby too!"

"Well, you can't have one," said Michelle firmly. "I expect you'll have lots of babies when you're grown-up, but you can't have one now."

"But I want one now!" roared Colette.

"You can't, duckie," explained Peronelle gently. "It isn't possible."

"Why not?" yelled Colette.

"Because you've got to have a husband before you have a baby, and only grown-up people have husbands."

"But I don't want a husband!" shouted Colette. "I want a baby!"

"Oh, be quiet, do!" implored Michelle. "Blow her nose, someone, for heaven's sake!"

"You're nothing but a baby yourself, Colette," scoffed Colin. "A nasty little red-faced cry-baby whose nose wants wiping."

At this, but for Michelle, there would have been a

battle. "Stop it!" she commanded, pushing them apart. "Horrid little children! How are we to get those lanterns made if you spend the whole afternoon scrapping?"

They ran across the courtyard, everything forgotten except the night's adventure and the preparations for it. "Come on!" they yelled to each other. "The stable and the mangel-wurzels! The carols! Get the kitchen cushions and the rug from Michelle's bed and come *on*!"

The du Frocqs had an even greater capacity than most children for changing in the space of half a minute from demons to angels, and vice versa. There was still a slight suggestion of tails and cloven hoofs about them as they lifted the latch of the stable door, but the moment it had clicked shut behind them they were all wing and halo. Their eyes beamed softly in the dim light and they smiled at each other as though family disagreement was a thing unknown.

This happy transformation could perhaps partly be attributed to the influence of the stable itself, for a stable is a delightful place at any time, but on Christmas Eve it moves quietly from its usual position on the fringe of human life and becomes the hub of the world.

The moment they had shut the door behind them the children knew that some strange change had come over their stable as well as over themselves. Outwardly it looked just the same, with its raftered cobwebby roof from which hung a lantern and bunches of dried herbs, and those lovely orange seed-pods that children call

Chinese lanterns, its uneven floor of rounded cobbles, its little square window through which the sunshine shone slantwise like a golden sword, and its dark velvety shadows that were not frightening shadows, like those in the lanes at midnight, but deep cool wells of comfort and friendliness. And it smelt just the same; of the sweet fresh hay in the mangers, of oats and clean horses and dried herbs; a smell of field and gardens that almost set high summer blazing in mid-winter.

And the animals looked as usual; Lupin, the old fat horse who pulled the family carriage; Mathilde, the sprightly piebald person who did the milk round in the mornings; Albert, Grandpapa's little donkey who had been lent to them over Christmas; Olivia, the lovely little fawn-coloured Jersey cow, who had not been well lately and so had been promoted from the cow byre to the stable; Maximilian, their plump black mongrel dog; and Marmalade the cat, who was ensconced in a box beneath Lupin's manger with a family of six ginger kits.

And yet it was all quite different. The motes of dust in the golden beam of sun were dancing with ecstasy, the hay in the manger was whispering and rustling as though it had secrets to tell, and the comfortable shadows had mysteries in their depths.

And the animals were in a queer mood; aloof, even a little patronizing. The night-black eyes of Lupin and Mathilde were as mysterious as the shadows, and Albert the donkey, usually so meek, was brandishing his tail and stamping his hoofs as though he, and not the lion, were the king of beasts. Maximilian, though he lay quite still with his nose on his extended paws and his silky black lids a little lowered over his lustrous eyes, was yet quivering with excitement, and the yellow eyes of Marmalade, sitting royally among her squirming kits, shone like lamps.

The children, with Michelle's rug over them, settled themselves comfortably on the cushions and a pile of hay in the one empty stall, with their backs turned to the empty manger, and set to work on their mangel-wurzels, making little windows in their sides with their pocket knives and scooping out places in the middle for the candles to stand. As they worked they sang, Peronelle beating time and leading them in a voice that had a blackbird's sweetness but unfortunately not a blackbird's capacity for sticking to the right note. Regarded as a musical performance their carol singing was hardly a success, for they none of them had an ear for music and each sang in a different key, but the stable liked it. . . . The hay stopped whispering to listen, the shadows crept a little closer and the animals looked up over their shoulders with softly beaming eyes. . . . They sang Good King Wenceslas, Noel and While Shepherds Watched, and they sang too, in their Island patois, some of the old cradle songs that had been crooned to them when they were babies, and the French carols they had learnt in the nuns' kindergarten where they had gone when they were little.

It was not until they had finished singing that they commented to each other upon the strangeness of the stable, and then only very tentatively, each afraid that the others would laugh at what they all were feeling.

"It's a nice old legend," said Michelle airily.

"What?" asked Peronelle, though she knew quite well what Michelle was thinking of.

"That all stables are changed and sacred on Christmas Eve.   That at midnight, in every stable all over the Island, the animals kneel down and worship the manger."

This was an old belief on the Island, and had lasted for hundreds of years.   The peasants and little children believed it, and the grown-up intellectuals, smiling tolerantly, were careful not to smudge it with the breath of their own disbelief.

"Wouldn't it be fun," said Colin, "to be here at midnight, in our own stable, and see what happens."

"No! No!" cried Jacqueline in horror.   "You know quite well, Colin, that any human being who dares to look at the animals at midnight falls down dead."

Though this also was part of the legend they all, except Colette, who was busy playing some game of her own in the shadows, roared with laughter at her, so that she hung her head in rosy shame. . . . Only the animals did not laugh.   Lupin and Mathilde, looking over their shoulders again, whinnied softly and warningly, and Albert, flinging up his head, ee-hawed like a trumpet blast.

"Whatever's the matter with Albert?" asked Colin. "You'd think he owned the whole place."

"Donkeys are always conceited on Christmas Eve," explained Peronelle softly.   "You see, one of them carried Mary when she rode to Bethlehem."

"I wonder what Albert will do to-night at midnight," mused Colin.   "It's all nonsense about falling down dead. I say, you girls, let's get back from the carol singing when midnight is striking and look."

"Ye—es," said Michelle doubtfully. "Perhaps just *after* midnight."

"Yes," decided Peronelle briskly. "After midnight. It's a pity to run unnecessary risks. Though there's nothing in it, of course."

"Oh, nothing," said Michelle airily. "Surely we've done enough lanterns now? It must be teatime. Come on. Where's Colette?"

So absorbed had they been in their mangel-wurzels that they had not noticed that Colette had left them. Now, turning round, they saw her behind them at the empty manger.

She had filled it with fresh hay and decorated it all round the edge with herbs and orange Chinese lanterns that she had pulled from low-hanging bunches, and now she had climbed right inside it and was pressing the hay with her fat hands and her dimpled knees to make a soft place in the middle. The last of the after-noon sun, shining full upon her, illumined her blue frock and touched her golden curls to a flaming aureole.

"She's like a bird preparing a nest, isn't she?" whispered Michelle. "Little birds sit inside their nests like that and press them with their bodies to make them round."

"She's like a little angel," said Peronelle softly, and felt a pang at her heart, for there were times when her little sister seemed to her so saintly that she was afraid she would spread her wings and fly away back to heaven.

But Colin had no such illusions.

"Teatime, Colette," he roared at her.

Colette's round face popped up over the edge of the manger. "What's for tea?" she demanded.

"Muffins," said Colin. "Toasted . . . Mother told me . . . and gâche."

Gâche was a particularly ravishing kind of Island cake much beloved by Colette. She rolled over the edge of the manger like a cherub falling from heaven, picked herself up and trundled eagerly towards the door.

"Come on," she cried to the others, standing on tip-toe to lift the latch. "Gâche. Muffins. Come *on*."

Reassured, they came on, taking their noise and laughter with them across the snow-covered courtyard to the old farmhouse where the lamp was already lit behind the kitchen window, and the kettle was singing beside the hearth. . . . The stable was left to a silence so deep that the rustle of the hay and the soft rhythm of the animals' breathing were only audible as heart-beats throbbing at the centre of the world.

It was moments such as this one, thought Rachell du Frocq, the mother of the children, as she lifted the old silver teapot in her beautiful hands, that justified life. . . . It was moments like this that made it worth while. . . . Her eyes passed caressingly over the bright heads of the munching children and met those of André her husband, sitting opposite to her at the old kitchen table, and he nodded, reading her thought.

They were an attractive couple. Rachell, beautiful,

strong-willed, tall and proud, with dark hair coiled on her shapely head like a coronet and black eyes whose indomitable fire neither sickness, sorrow or hardship had ever been known to quench; and André, thin, bearded, deprecating, a dreamy idealist who put his ideals into practice in private life with such success that his gentle unselfishness more than made up to his family for his complete lack of any practical ability whatsoever.

Their eyes, having met and greeted each other, looked lovingly at the room where they sat, an old room that had absorbed the joy and peace of some three hundred Christmas Eves into the pulse of its life. The log fire was burning brightly in the great chimney enclosure, with its stone seats one on each side and its bread oven built in the thickness of the wall. It flickered its dancing light over the whitewashed, raftered ceiling, the *jonquiere* or day-bed, the willow pattern china on the old oak dresser and the rich red and blue and gold of Rachell's best French teaset that was used only at festivals and birthdays. . . . A lovely room, warm and companionable and, just for this once, for the children never spoke when muffins and gâche were on the table, silent.

But silence never lasts long on a farm, and this one was shattered by the sudden, clattering entrance of Matthieu Torode, their milkman and mainstay on the farm, come to wish them good night before he tramped off to his lonely cottage on the cliffs. He was a nice person, was Matthieu, young and tall and broad-shouldered, with clod-hopping feet that could yet tread very gently when a cow was sick, and large ugly hands that could milk with a swiftness and skill unrivalled on the Island. He was an inarticulate person but what little he did say was always rich with the courtesy of the Island peasant, and his bright dark eyes and sudden smile were as vividly alive as water flashing beneath the sun.

"Good night, M'sieur, M'dame, Mamselles," he said. "*Dieu vous garde.*"

"Good night!" they cried. "Merry Christmas, Matthieu, merry Christmas!"

"Merry Christmas!" he echoed, his dark eyes suddenly sombre, and bowing he left them rather abruptly, banging the door.

"So lonely in that cottage of his!" murmured Rachell compassionately. "That wretched girl!"

For two years ago Matthieu, so large and capable and seemingly full of common sense, had allowed himself to be made a fool of by a slip of a girl whose head did not even reach to the top of his shoulder. She was Denise Marquand, the granddaughter of the eccentric, savage old farmer who owned Blanchelande, the desolate farm upon a cliff-top not two miles from them, and when Matthieu triumphantly announced his betrothal to her Rachell shook her head in gloomy prophecy. She did not know Denise, who had only a few weeks before come from her convent school in France to live with her grandfather, but the name Marquand was an ominous one on the Island, for the Marquands were no good. They had never been any good, and their farm had for centuries been shunned by the Islanders. The present owner of it, and the last man to bear the name of Marquand, old Alexander Marquand, returned the compliment. . . . He set his dogs upon any but his own labourers who ventured near Blanchelande. . . . He was not even neighbourly with the du Frocqs, though friendship between Bon Repos and Blanchelande was an old tradition. In business matters he had for years been rewarding André's fair play with double dealing, and his friendly greetings with black looks, and gradually all intercourse between the two had wilted and died. So no one from Bon Repos except Matthieu, who had wooed her on the cliffs when the gorse was out in the spring and the primroses were turning every sheltered hollow into a cup of sweetness, had ever set eyes on Denise when she eloped to France with some idle, handsome, holiday-making Frenchman whom she met down on the sands below her home.

Strange stories were told of the old man's rage, of the vow he had made to set the dogs on her too if she ever dared to show her face at Blanchelande again, but no corroboration of them could ever be got out of Matthieu. . . . He never mentioned the name Marquand again. . . . He gave all his tenderness and strength to the farm animals, no doubt finding, like many another man before him, that the more he saw of loquacious human beings the more he preferred dumb animals.

"He's not got over it," said Rachell to André, recalling Matthieu's sombre look and sudden exit.

"Surely," said André. "It was two years ago."

"Two years," said Rachell, "though they may pass like two centuries, do not heal a wound."

"No," agreed André sadly.

"May we get down?" asked Colin, uninterested by this discussion. "We've eaten everything and we have several important things to do."

"Of course," smiled Rachell. "There is silver paper and ribbon for tying up the presents in my bottom drawer."

It was when the children had gone, and she and André sat one on each side of the glowing fire, that the knock came at the front door. They went together to open it, expecting it to be some friend come to wish them a happy Christmas, and together they stared in astonishment at the slim girl with her baby in her arms.

"Can you give me some food?" she demanded, and her clear, imperious voice was in such contrast to her beggar-maid clothes that for the moment they were rooted to the spot. She swept past them, across the hall and into the lighted kitchen, where she dropped down on one of the benches within the chimney enclosure and unwound her shawl from her sleeping baby.

"I've enough money left to pay for a night's lodging," she said, when her hosts had pulled themselves together sufficiently to follow her, "but I'd like food and a rest before I look for it. I'm tired. I crossed from France to-day."

The shawl had fallen back from her beautiful little head and showed her white face drawn with fatigue,

214

with the dark eyes deeply shadowed but as indomitable as Rachell's own.

"Oh, and could you lend me a needle and thread," she went on. "My skirt's torn."

On one side it hung in jagged rents round her ankles, and Rachell exclaimed at the sight of it. "You fell?" she asked.

"No," said the girl briefly. "At the place where I went some dogs were set on me," and brushing André's ejaculations of horror contemptuously aside she reached eagerly for the food that he brought her.

While Rachell nursed the adorable baby she ate as greedily as a little child, now and then vouchsafing them a little information between her eager mouthfuls.

"I chose this house to come to because I liked your children," she said.

"You saw the children?" asked André.

"I met them in the lane this afternoon. Nice children. The children of good parents."

"This baby," said Rachell, rocking her knee, "has a good parent. I've never seen so clean a baby."

"Almost the last of my money," smiled the girl, "went on soap and baby powder."

Rachell looked up, her eyes on the black clothes. "You are widowed?" she asked gently.

"Yes, Madame," replied the girl. "But that is not a matter for condolence."

The sudden hardness of her tone, and the defiant fling back of her head, made André wince. They opened a door upon a blackness of sordid disillusion

215

upon which one hated to look on Christmas Eve. "That is past," he said hastily. "That is past."

"Thank God," said the girl, and reached for another piece of cake.

It was when she had finished it, and was preparing for departure, that there began between Rachell and André one of those wordless battles of the will which their differences of temperament made amusingly frequent. . . . For André was one of those idealists who stick at nothing; he would have given his last shilling to a beggar at the door and gone to bed perfectly happy in the conviction that God would provide for his starving family in the morning. . . . Rachell, on the other hand, believed that charity began at home; she would have given the half of her last shilling to the beggar at the door and gone to bed happy in the conviction that at least she had sixpence left for the children's breakfast should it turn out that, after all, there is no God.

So now André, with a flicker of his left eyelid, a half gesture of his head towards the *jonquire* and a whole gesture of his right thumb towards the ceiling, suggested to Rachell that Colin should be put to sleep in the kitchen to-night and his little room given to this mother and child.

But Rachell received these hints with no signs of enthusiasm. . . . She knew nothing about this girl. . . . She was not going to have her in the house with her innocent daughters. . . . With a swift, cool glance she put André in his place and turned back to the girl.

"They will give you a bed at a fisherman's cottage I

know of at the hamlet of Breton Bay," she said kindly, but with the utmost firmness. "The woman is an old servant of mine and I will write a note saying that I have sent you. To-morrow I will come down and see you and you will tell me how I can help you."

Obediently, though her face was a little sullen, the girl rose, holding out her arms for her baby.

André tried once more. . . . He coughed, poked the fire, laid a gentle hand upon his wife's shoulder. . . . All no good.

"You will find the way quite easily," continued Rachell evenly, just as though he had neither coughed nor poked. "Take the lane to the right at the cross roads and go straight on."

"I know the way," said the girl proudly. . . . So proudly that André knew she did not want, beggar-maid though she was, to stoop to the humility of seeking for shelter at Breton Bay.

"That's right," said Rachell heartily. "Sit down again, my dear, while I write the note, and wrap up a few comforts for you and the babe."

André, beaten and sorrowful, turned and went out. As he slammed the front door behind him, and stood in the snowy courtyard looking up at the blazing stars, a voice tolled over and over again in his brain: "There was no room for them in the inn."

Slowly he crossed the courtyard to the stable, for it was time he lit the oil stove that kept his beloved animals warm through the night. His thoughts reached out to them in a glow of affection, for according to the

o 217

Island legend to-night was their hour of glory of which
no man might defraud them.

With a little thrill at his heart he lifted the latch and
walked in. The silver starlight softly illumined the
stable and showed him the patient shapes of the
animals, their breath hanging like incense in the
fragrant air. Maximilian, running to him, kissed his
hand and folded an affectionate black body round his
right leg.

"So you're here, old chap, are you?" said André,
pulling the silky ears. "Why aren't you in the house?
Why are you neglecting your family on Christmas
Eve?"

Maximilian squirmed his body apologetically and
André suddenly remembered that he always did leave
the house for the stable on Christmas Eve. . . . Their
dogs always had. . . . Odd.

Dismissing the oddness he fumbled for matches and
bent to light the oil stove that stood in the empty stall.
It was good to see its soft golden light creep tentatively
out into the mysterious shadows, laying caressing fingers
of light on the animals' satiny backs and—what was
that?—lighted candles set around the empty manger?

He started and came nearer, then stood gazing, not
ashamed of a pricking behind his eyelids as he looked at
Colette's Chinese lanterns, set like tapering flames about
the manger where her hands had pressed the hay to
make the nest within it soft and round.

Half in play and half in earnest, a little ashamed but
yet enjoying himself, he set to work to complete the
preparations that she had begun. He tidied the stable,

sweeping up the scattered hay and putting in a tidy pile the rug and cushions that the children had left in disarray when they stampeded off to tea, and finally he lighted the lamp so that it swung like a star from the raftered ceiling. Then, with one long last look round, he went softly out into the courtyard and neglected, purposely, or in forgetfulness, he hardly knew which, to lock the door behind him.

A beam of lantern light, shining out from the stable door before he closed it, showed him a figure standing in the shadows beside the doorway to the lane. . . . So she was too proud, after all, to obey Rachell and seek shelter with a fisherman's wife? . . . He crossed the snowy courtyard hastily, yet when he got to the door he found he had been mistaken, for there was no one there.

"Has the poor girl gone, dear?" he asked Rachell when he returned to the kitchen.

"Ages ago, darling," replied Rachell cheerfully. "You've been an unconscionable time in that stable. . . . It was quite impossible, dearest, for me to have a girl like that in the house with the girls. . . . I know best in these matters."

André gave the little dignified gesture of the head with which his side of an argument always ended; a gesture that admitted the right of her stronger will to its own way but kept his own opinion unaltered. Then, gently changing the subject, he began to tell her about Colette's manger.

Some hours later, in the snowy lane, the children

stood together in a little group, palpitating with excitement. Everything had worked out according to plan. They had gone obediently to bed and then they had got up again and left the house by way of Peronelle's bedroom window and the back-door porch. They stood now lighting the candle ends in their lanterns, and exclaiming in delight as the points of flame steadied into glowing petals of gold that spread their radiance over the strange world of glistening snow and silvered trees whose tops were lost in the blackness of the night.

"Where are we going first?" asked Michelle.

"Blanchelande," replied Colin promptly.

He had expected an outcry from the girls, for the farm of Alexander Marquand was "out of bounds". . . . Rachell, though she thought it likely that the grim stories told about the old man had in them more falsehood than truth, was yet taking no chances for the children. . . . But there was no outcry, only a quickly drawn breath of excitement. The girls, apparently, thought as he did, that in this magical star-lit night their destination must be a fairy-tale one; if not Aladdin's cave then an ogre's castle; and no place has a greater fairy-tale quality than a forbidden house where fear dwells.

The only dissentient voice was Peronelle's. "Won't it be too far for Colette?" she asked a little anxiously.

"If it is you girls can carry her," said Colin.

At this the girls looked a little askance at Colette, for the addition of two coats, gaiters and a woollen muffler to her already immense collection of underclothes had made her broader than she was long, and correspondingly heavy. Moreover, she had had to be awakened from sleep to be brought on this expedition and was still drowsy with it, her golden head in its red tam-o'-shanter so heavy with dreams that it was lolling on her neck like an overweighted dahlia.

"Carry her yourself," said the girls indignantly to Colin.

"Not me," said Colin.

"Not going to be carried," lisped Colette indignantly between two yawns. "Colette walk."

"Come on, then," said Colin. "Step out. It's a goodish way."

It certainly was, but so wonderful a way that no one grumbled. They chose the cliff path to Blanchelande, where they were out in the open, rather than the inland lane where who-knew-what lurked in the shadows under the trees. It took them past Matthieu Torode's little cottage, tucked away cosily in a hollow where in spring the gorse and the broom were a blaze of gold, and on along the cliff-top, with the sea murmuring against the rocks far down below them, and over their heads a great sky set with blazing stars, and a round white moon whose light made a glittering pathway over the sea and illumined the fallen snow with points of spark-ling fire.

It had not been a heavy fall and it did not clog their footsteps; it was a white crisp coverlet that smoothed their path for them and beckoned them on and on for the sheer joy of printing their footsteps in its whiteness, waiting for them as the virgin page waits for the im-print of the poet's mind upon it.

"Look what we've written!" said Jacqueline, with a backward glance over her shoulder. "What does it say?"

"Peace and goodwill," said Peronelle softly. "Look! Here is Blanchelande."

The farm was true to its name on a night like this. Between the white moonlight and the white snow its gaunt granite walls gleamed like white marble. It stood foursquare to the winds, with no trees to shelter it and no creepers veiling the hardness of its outlines. There were no lights in the windows and no smoke rising from the chimney, and behind it the farm buildings crouched like frightened animals. . . . It might have been a house where only the ghosts were alive.

If the children's hearts failed them a little they gave no sign. Resolutely they made their way to the front of the house, where a door of such strength and grimness that it seemed to defy all entry faced a courtyard littered with garbage and untidy boxes and barrels.

"Now," said Peronelle. "Do we sing out here, or knock at the door and ask to go in?"

But no one answered her question for suddenly, as though the gates of hell had been opened, pandemonium broke out in such a fury of barking and baying and snarling as the children had never heard. . . . They had forgotten the Blanchelande dogs. . . . They came streaking out from behind the house, and from the shadows of the courtyard, their leaping gliding bodies dark against the snow. . . . There were at least a hundred of them.

"Steady, you chaps," said Peronelle's quiet, courageous voice. "Stand together with Colette in the middle. Keep your heads and remember that dogs always like us and we like dogs."

Dogs? But were these dogs? They seemed more like wolves. Though their heads were up and they would sooner have died than run away the heart of each child turned to water within it.

"There are only four," said Peronelle, counting. "Speak to them very politely and hold out your fists for them to smell."

"Good dogs," murmured the du Frocqs courageously. "A merry Christmas. Peace and Goodwill. We're only carol singers and we don't mean any harm," and they bravely held out their doubled fists to the snarling jaws.

The dogs lifted their inquiring noses to the fists and smelt them, they lowered them to the hems of the children's coats and smelt those, they cocked their ears to the sounds of the children's voices and gazed with deep absorption at their boots. They were satisfied. These were good children. They smelt courageous and sounded kind-hearted and their boots were respectable boots. Four pink tongues curled out to caress and four tails were raised in welcome.

"Hi! You get out of there!"

The door had been flung open and a harsh voice was shouting at them from the dark cavern within.

"We're carol singers," explained Peronelle. "We're coming inside to sing to you."

"Oh, are you?" inquired the voice grimly. "Not if I know it. You get along home or I'll set the dogs on you."

"You can't," said Colin. "The dogs like us."

The voice materialized into a tall stooping figure that came out into the moonlight and confronted them, and for the first time the children looked up into the face of the hated Alexander Marquand. He was an old man, fierce-eyed, grey-bearded, with a lean weather-beaten face that seemed to have been carved in keen fierce lines out of a piece of dark wood. . . . Yet the children, who had never yet met cruelty in any form, felt no fear of him. . . . They smiled engagingly.

"Let us in," they pleaded.

Hands in pockets he surveyed them, the moonlight and lantern light illuminating for him their glowing pink cheeks and bright eyes and delightfully bunchy figures, and the dogs standing round them with sterns a-quiver and eyes raised beseechingly to their master's face. . . . Let these children in, they said, for they smell right.

But it was Colette, tired out by the walk along the cliff, who clinched the matter. Both her father and her grandfather had grey beards and the very sight of one recalled to her mind strong arms that in her baby-hood had lifted her off her inadequate legs—Colette's legs had never been equal to her weight—and a personality from whom emanated all the good things of this life. She ran to Monsieur Marquand, clasping him with her fat hands, her cherubic face raised to him, imploring warmth, shelter, and an opportunity of sitting down. "My legs ache," she said.

Before he realized what he was doing he had picked her up and carried her into his dark stone-floored kitchen, the dogs and the other children following pell-mell at his heels, and set her down before the dying fire, staring at the lot of them in comical bewilderment.

But the children knew quite well what to do. They pushed Monsieur Marquand into his fireside chair and gave him Colette to hold upon his knees, they flung wood upon the dying embers and lit the oil lamp that hung from the rafters. They took chestnuts from their pockets—chestnuts were a very important part of Christmas fare on the Island and every child's pocket was full of them—and set them to roast upon the hearth-stone, and then sitting down cross-legged before the fire they began to sing.

The years rolled away from Alexander Marquand. All his bitterness and hatred, his inheritance from a line of savage forbears and fostered in him by years of misfortune and bereavement, seemed to be going with the smoke up the chimney. The kitchen that a short while ago had seemed cold, empty and dark was filled with warmth and light, singing and the cheerful sound of popping chestnuts. Old memories awoke and peopled it with ghosts; the figures of his childhood, the brothers and sisters who more than a half-century ago had sung these very same French carols; his own dead children, who had roasted their chestnuts at this hearthstone; his little granddaughter who used to sit upon his knee as Colette was sitting now. . . . A bitter memory this last one. His pride would never forgive her for the disgrace she had brought upon his name.

"I think we ought to be going now," said one of the

children suddenly, after a long while. "You see, we want to be home by midnight, so as to look in the stable afterwards and see if the animals are still kneeling down."

Monsieur Marquand started and looked up. For how long had he been sitting here, eating chestnuts, listening to carols, dreaming dreams and seeing visions? The child, he was astonished to find, was now asleep in his arms, her golden head on his shoulder. So bewildered was he that he was not quite certain what child it was; one of his own out of the past or some cherub out of the carols the children had been singing; in either case he was reluctant to let it go.

"I'll come with you," he said, "and carry the child."

The homeward journey was as magical as the outward one, perhaps more magical because of the tremendous waiting silence that gripped the world. . . . The sea was hardly whispering now and the blaze of the stars seemed a little veiled, as though they had hidden their eyes. . . . The old man and the children plodded on, the four dogs at their heels, and none of them spoke until they were nearly home and saw three figures with a swinging lantern coming to meet them.

"Mother and Father and Matthieu Torode!" ejaculated Michelle. "But how did they know where we were?"

"They went up to fill our stockings and found us gone," said Peronelle. "Idiots that we were not to think of that!"

"They fetched out Matthieu to help them and tracked our footsteps through the snow!" exclaimed Colin. "Well done them! Hullo, Father! Hullo, Mother!"

"You naughty children!" cried Rachell, thoroughly exasperated now that her anxiety was relieved. "I'd like to spank the lot of you."

"You have made your Mother very anxious," reproved André mildly.

Suddenly Matthieu, who had been grinning jovially and swinging the lantern, saw who it was who carried Colette. "Monsieur Marquand!" he ejaculated, and the smile was wiped off his face and his lantern became rigid.

"Monsieur Marquand?" asked André and Rachell, and gazed in astonishment at the man who for years had so unreasonably counted himself their enemy.

Monsieur Marquand made a move as though to put Colette into her mother's arms. "May I restore your property to you, Madame," he said coldly. "And then bid you good night."

"No, Marquand!" said André sharply. "You have done us a service to-night and you will come home and have a drink with me."

Monsieur Marquand hesitated, and made another effort to dislodge Colette, but she was comfortable where she was and wriggled closer. With a curt, abrupt nod he yielded.

The first stroke of midnight, borne very faintly on the still air from the distant town of St. Pierre, rang out as the cavalcade entered the courtyard. It was followed by bell after bell, as all the different church clocks in the town began to strike, so far away that the tiny sounds seemed like tinkling drops of water falling into the deep well of the gripping silence. The little group of human beings halted, as though a hand had been laid on them to quiet their shuffling feet and wagging tongues, but the four Marquand dogs went like a streak of lightning across the snowy courtyard, and the foremost one, making a little crying noise like an eager child, pushed his nose against the door; it must have been unlatched because it opened a little way, letting out a beam of light that stretched right across the snow to the feet of the watching humans, and the four dogs went in.

The last stroke of midnight sounded from the last of the St. Pierre churches, there was a pause, and then, still so faint and far away that it sounded as though they were ringing under the sea, the Christmas bells rang out in silvery peals that seemed to the listeners to be the twinkling frost and the sparkling stars made audible in music.

"Now," said Colin softly, and with the now fully awakened Colette close at his heels he ran across to the stable door and flung it open.

He was not surprised, of course, and neither was Colette, though it was even lovelier than they had expected, but to all the others what they saw inside the stable had the quality of one of those blinding visions that change the whole course of a man's life for ever.

MIDNIGHT IN THE STABLE

229

All the animals had gathered round in a semicircle; the horses, the cow, the little donkey, the five dogs and the golden cat. They were not kneeling down now, though Colin stoutly declared afterwards that he had heard them get up from their knees when he opened the door. The dogs were lying with their noses on their paws and the other animals were standing quietly brooding, their wide dark eyes fixed on the baby who lay in the decorated manger, curled round fast asleep in the soft place that Colette's hands had pressed out. His pretty mother had been sleeping among the cushions that André had arranged so tidily on the hay, but she was sitting up now and rubbing the sleep out of her eyes. As they stood there watching she let her hands drop and looked up at them, smiling, her eyes dark with mystery in her flower-like face. The light of the lantern, swinging overhead, illumined the scene with a glowing softness that seemed strangely to come from the manger itself. . . . Each stalk of hay seemed a line of golden light and Colette's Chinese lanterns glowed round the crib like petals of flame. . . . The deep stillness in which they watched lasted for a few more minutes whose brief span seemed like eternity, and through it the bells threaded their silver chain of sound.

It was these minutes that the children remembered ever afterwards. It was this vision that was reality and not the swift tumult of following events that seemed to them to have the confusion of a dream and to be as little worthy of attention. . . . Yet a few details of the

dream stuck in their memory; Matthieu's cry of
"Denise! Denise!" a cry so full of grief and longing
that it pierced them as though an arrow had gone
through their bodies; Denise's face raised to his, white
with her mute passion of penitence; old Monsieur
Marquand most unaccountably bursting into tears and
being patted on the back by their father; Denise's
clear voice, restored to her at last, saying over and over
again: "Forgive me. Forgive me, Madame; I did not
want to go down to Breton Bay and so I crept into the
stable instead. Forgive me, Grandfather. Please,
Matthieu, forgive me. . . ." Monsieur Marquand
asked no one to forgive him, though goodness knew,
thought the children afterwards, his behaviour in
setting the dogs on Denise when she had tried to go
back to her home had been atrocious enough; but then
perhaps his tears, the first he had shed for sixty years,
so he said later, were a rich ransom for his evil
deeds.

So many things were ransomed by the events of that
night; the ancient friendship between Bon Repos and
Blanchelande; the old affection between Monsieur
Marquand and his granddaughter; the old love between
Matthieu and Denise that born again transformed her
into Madame Torode, a rosy-cheeked matron who lived
in the little cottage in the gorse-filled hollow on the
cliffs, and watched her son grow to strength and vigour
on an Island of peace and goodwill set like a jewel
between sun and sea.

But to the children Denise and her baby were not to
be identified with the mother and child they had seen

in the stable. No. These were eternal, unchanging figures. . . . A mother who would never grow old and a child who would never grow up. . . . The children would probably never see them again; but the animals would. Every Christmas Eve, when the church clocks of St. Pierre struck midnight, the animals would kneel down and worship what they saw.

PERONELLE

COLIN

MICHELLE